1 3 5 7 9 10 8 6 4 2

Vintage
20 Vauxhall Bridge Road,
London SW1V 2SA

Vintage Classics is part of the Penguin Random House
group of companies whose addresses can be found at
global.penguinrandomhouse.com.

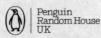

Penguin
Random House
UK

A Bunch of Fives was first published in Great Britain by
Vintage Classics in 2012

This short edition published by Vintage in 2017

penguin.co.uk/vintage

A CIP catalogue record for this book is available from the British Library

ISBN 9781784872731

Typeset in 9.5/14.5 pt FreightText Pro
by Jouve (UK), Milton Keynes
Printed and bound by Clays Ltd, St Ives plc

Penguin Random House is committed to a sustainable future for
our business, our readers and our planet. This book is made from
Forest Stewardship Council® certified paper.

MIX
Paper from
responsible sources
FSC® C018179
www.fsc.org

Motherhood

HELEN SIMPSON

VINTAGE MINIS

Lentils and Lilies

JADE BEAUMONT WAS TECHNICALLY UP in her bedroom revising for the A levels which were now only weeks away. Her school gave them study days at home, after lectures on trust and idleness. She was supposed to be sorting out the differences between Wordsworth and Coleridge at the moment.

Down along the suburban pleasantness of Miniver Road the pavements were shaded by fruit trees, and the front gardens of the little Edwardian villas smiled back at her with early lilac, bushes of crimson flowering currant and the myopic blue dazzle of forget-me-nots. She felt light on her feet and clever, like a cat, snuffing the air, pinching a pungent currant leaf.

There was a belief held by Jade's set that the earlier you hardened yourself off and bared your skin, the more lasting the eventual tan; and so she had that morning pulled on a brief white skirt and T-shirt. She was on her way to an interview for a holiday job at the garden centre. Summer!

She couldn't wait. The morning was fair but chilly and the white-gold hairs on her arms and legs stood up and curved to form an invisible reticulation, trapping a layer of warm air a good centimetre deep.

> I may not hope from outward forms to win
> The passion and the life, whose fountains are within.

That was cool, but Coleridge was a minefield. Just when you thought he'd said something really brilliant, he went raving off full steam ahead into nothingness. He was a nightmare to write about. Anyway, she herself found outward forms utterly absorbing, the colour of clothes, the texture of skin, the smell of food and flowers. She couldn't see the point of extrapolation. Keats was obviously so much better than the others, but you didn't get the choice of questions with him.

She paused to inhale the sweet air around a philadelphus Belle Etoile, then noticed the host of tired daffodils at its feet.

> Shades of the prison-house begin to close
> Upon the growing boy,
> But he beholds the light, and whence it flows,
> He sees it in his joy.

She looked back down her years at school, the reined-in feeling, the stupors of boredom, the teachers in the classrooms like tired lion-tamers, and felt quite the opposite.

She was about to be let out. And every day when she left the house, there was the excitement of being noticed, the warmth of eye-beams, the unfolding consciousness of her own attractive powers. She was the focus of every film she saw, every novel she read. She was about to start careering round like a lustrous loose cannon.

> Full soon thy soul shall have her earthly freight,
> And custom lie upon thee with a weight,
> Heavy as frost, and deep almost as life!

She was never going to go dead inside or live somewhere boring like this, and she would make sure she was in charge at any work she did and not let it run her. She would never be like her mother, making rotas and lists and endless arrangements, lost forever in a forest of twitching detail with her tense talk of juggling and her self-importance about her precious job and her joyless 'running the family'. No, life was not some sort of military campaign; or, at least, *hers* would not be.

When she thought of her mother, she saw tendons and hawsers, a taut figure at the front door screaming at them all to do their music practice. She was always off out; she made them do what she said by remote control. Her trouble was, she'd forgotten how to relax. It was no wonder Dad was like he was.

And everybody said she was so amazing, what she managed to pack into twenty-four hours. Dad worked hard, they said, but she worked hard too *and* did the home shift,

She would never be like her mother, making rotas and lists and endless arrangements

whatever that was. Not really so very amazing though; she'd forgotten to get petrol a couple of weeks ago, and the school run had ground to a halt. In fact some people might say downright inefficient.

On the opposite side of the road, a tall girl trailed past with a double buggy of grizzling babies, a Walkman's shrunken tinkling at her ears. Au pair, remarked Jade expertly to herself, scrutinising the girl's shoes, cerise plastic jellies set with glitter. She wanted some just like that, but without the purple edging.

She herself had been dragged up by a string of au pairs. Her mother hated it when she said that. After all, she *was* supposed to take delight in us! thought Jade viciously, standing stock-still, outraged; like, *be* there with us. For us. Fair seed-time had my soul I *don't* think.

Above her the cherry trees were fleecy and packed with a foam of white petals. Light warm rays of the sun reached her upturned face like kisses, refracted as a fizzy dazzle through the fringing of her eyelashes. She turned to the garden beside her and stared straight into a magnolia tree, the skin of its flowers' stiff curves streaked with a sexual crimson. She was transported by the light and the trees, and just as her child self had once played the miniature warrior heroine down green alleys, so she saw her self now floating in this soft sunshine, moving like a panther into the long jewelled narrative which was her future.

Choice landscapes and triumphs and adventures quivered, quaintly framed there in the zigzag light like pendant crystals on a chandelier. There was the asterisk trail of a shooting star, on and on for years until it petered out at about thirty-three or thirty-four, leaving her at some point of self-apotheosis, high and nobly invulnerable, one of Tiepolo's ceiling princesses looking down in beautiful amusement from a movie-star cloud. This was about as far as any of the novels and films took her too.

A pleasurable sigh escaped her as the vision faded, and she started walking again, on past the tranquil houses, the coloured glass in a hall window staining the domestic light, a child's bicycle propped against the trunk of a standard rose. She sensed babies breathing in cots in upstairs rooms, and solitary women becalmed somewhere downstairs, chopping fruit or on the telephone organising some toddler tea. It really was suburban purdah round here. They were like battery hens, weren't they, rows of identical hutches, so neat and tidy and narrow-minded. Imagine staying in all day, stewing in your own juices. Weren't they bored out of their skulls? It was beyond her comprehension.

And so materialistic, she scoffed, observing the pel-metted strawberry-thief curtains framing a front room window; so bourgeois. Whereas her gap-year cousin had just been all over India for under £200.

> The world is too much with us; late and soon,
> Getting and spending, we lay waste our powers.
> Little we see in Nature that is ours;
> We have given our hearts away, a sordid boon!

Although after a good patch of freedom she fully intended to pursue a successful career, the way ahead paved by her future degree in Business Studies. But she would never end up anywhere like here. No! It would be a converted warehouse with semi-astral views and no furniture. Except perhaps for the ultimate sofa.

Jade rounded the corner into the next road, and suddenly there on the pavement ahead of her was trouble. A child was lying flat down on its back screaming while a man in a boilersuit crouched over it, his anti-dust mask lifted to his forehead like a frogman. Above them both stood a broad fair woman, urgently advising the child to calm down.

'You'll be better with a child than I am,' said the workman gratefully as Jade approached, and before she could agree – or disagree – he had shot off back to his sand-blasting.

'She's stuck a lentil up her nose,' said the woman crossly, worriedly. 'She's done it before. More than once. I've got to get it out.'

She waved a pair of eyebrow tweezers in the air. Jade glanced down at the chubby blubbering child, her small squat nose and mess of tears and mucus, and moved away uneasily.

'We're always down at Casualty,' said the mother, as rapidly desperate as a talentless stand-up comedian. 'Last week she swallowed a penny. Casualty said, a penny's OK, wait for it to come out the other end. Which it did. But they'd have had to open her up if it had been a five-pence piece, something to do with the serration or the size. Then she pushed a drawing pin up her nose. They were worried it might get into her brain. But she sneezed it out. One time she even pushed a chip up her nostril, really far, and it needed extracting from the sinus tubes.'

Jade gasped fastidiously and stepped back.

'Maybe we should get her indoors,' suggested the woman, her hand on Jade's arm. 'It's that house there across the road.'

'I don't think . . .' started Jade.

'The baby, oh the baby!' yelped the woman. 'He's in the car. I forgot. I'll have to . . .'

Before Jade could escape, the woman was running like an ostrich across the road towards a blue Volvo, its passenger door open onto the pavement, where from inside came the sobbing of the strapped-in baby. Jade tutted, glancing down at her immaculate clothes, but she had no option really but to pick up the wailing child and follow the mother. She did not want to be implicated in the flabby womany-ness of the proceedings, and stared crossly at this overweight figure ahead of her, ludicrously top-heavy in its bulky stained sweatshirt and sagging leggings.

Closer up, in the hallway, her hyperaesthetic teenage eyes observed the mother's ragged cuticles, the graceless way her heels stuck out from the backs of her sandals like hunks of Parmesan, and the eyes which had dwindled to dull pinheads. The baby in her arms was dark red as a crab apple from bellowing, but calmed down when a bottle was plugged into its mouth.

It was worse in the front room. Jade lowered her snuffling burden to the carpet and looked around her with undisguised disdain. The furniture was all boring and ugly while the pictures, well the pictures were like a propaganda campaign for family values – endless groupings on walls and ledges and shelves of wedding pictures and baby photos, a fluttery white suffocation of clichés.

The coffee table held a flashing ansaphone and a hideous orange Amaryllis lily on its last legs, red-gold anthers shedding pollen. Jade sat down beside it and traced her initials in this yolk-yellow dust with her fingertip.

'I used to love gardening,' said the woman, seeing this. 'But there's no time now. I've got an Apple up in the spare room, I try to keep a bit of part-time going during their naps. Freelance PR. Typing CVs.'

She waved the tweezers again and knelt above her daughter on the carpet.

I wouldn't let you loose on my CV, thought Jade, recoiling. Not in a million years. It'd come back with jam all over it.

The little girl was quite a solid child and tried to control her crying, allowing herself to be comforted in between the probings inside her face. But she was growing hotter, and when, at the woman's request, Jade unwillingly held her, she was like a small combustion engine, full of distress.

'See, if I hold her down, you have a try,' said the woman, handing her the tweezers.

Jade was appalled and fascinated. She peered up the child's nose and could see a grey-green disc at the top of one fleshy nostril. Tentatively she waved the silver tongs. Sensibly the child began to howl. The mother clamped her head and shoulders down with tired violence.

'I don't think I'd better do this,' said Jade. She was frightened that metal inside the warm young face combined with sudden fierce movement could be a disastrous combination.

The woman tried again and the walls rang with her daughter's screams.

'Oh God,' she said. 'What can I do?'

'Ring your husband?' suggested Jade.

'He's in Leeds,' said the woman. 'Or is it Manchester. Oh dear.'

'Ha,' said Jade. You'd think it was the fifties, men roaming the world while the women stayed indoors. The personal was the political, hadn't she heard?

'I've got to make a phone call to say I'll be late,' said the woman, distracted yet listless. She seemed unable to think beyond the next few minutes or to formulate a plan of action, as though in a state of terminal exhaustion. Jade felt obscurely resentful. If she ever found herself in this sort of situation, a man, babies, etcetera; when the time came; IF. Well, he would be responsible for half the childcare and half the housework. At least. She believed in justice, unlike this useless great lump.

'Why don't you ring Casualty?' she suggested. 'See what the queues are like?'

'I did that before,' said the woman dully. 'They said, try to get it out yourself.'

'I'm sorry,' said Jade, standing up. 'I'm on my way to an interview. I'll be late if I stay.' People should deal with their own problems, she wanted to say; you shouldn't get yourself into situations you can't handle then slop all over everybody else.

'Yes,' said the woman. 'Thank you anyway.'

'You could ring the doctor,' said Jade on the way to the front door. 'Ask for an emergency appointment.'

'I'll do that next,' said the woman, brightening a little; then added suddenly, 'This year has been the hardest of my life. The two of them.'

'My mother's got four,' said Jade censoriously. '*And* a job. Goodbye.'

She turned with relief back into the shining spring morning and started to sprint, fast and light, as quick off the blocks as Atalanta.

Café Society

TWO SHATTERED WOMEN AND A bright-eyed child have just sat down at the window table in the café. Both women hope to talk, for their minds to meet; at the same time they are aware that the odds against this happening are about fifty to one. Still they have decided to back that dark horse Intimacy, somewhere out there muffledly galloping. They order coffee, and toast for the boy, who seizes a teaspoon and starts to bash away at the cracked ice marbling of the formica table.

'No, Ben,' says his mother, prising the spoon from his fingers and diverting his attention to the basket of sugar sachets. She flings discreet glances at the surrounding tables, gauging the degrees of irritability of those nearest. There are several other places they could have chosen, but this sandwich bar is where they came.

They might have gone to McDonald's, so cheap and tolerant, packed with flat light and fat smells and unofficial crèche clamour. There they could have slumped like the old punchbags they are while Ben screeched and flew around with the other children. McDonald's is essentially a wordless experience, though, and they both want to see if they can for a wonder exchange some words. Then there is Pete's Café on the main road, a lovely steamy unbuttoned room where men sit in their work clothes in a friendly fug of bonhomie and banter, smoking, stirring silver streams of sugar into mugs of bright brown tea. But it would not be fair to take this child in there and spoil that Edenic all-day-breakfast fun. It would take the insensitivity of an ox. Unthinkable.

Here is all right. They get all sorts here. Here is used to women walking in with that look on their faces – 'What hit me?' Even now there is a confused-looking specimen up there ordering a decaffeinated coffee, takeaway, at the counter.

'Every now and then I think I might give it up, see if that helps,' says Frances. 'Caffeine. But then I reckon it's just a drop in the ocean.'

Ben rocks backwards in his chair a few times, seeing how far he can go. He is making a resonant zooming noise behind his teeth, but not very loudly yet. Sally keeps her baggy eye on him and says, 'Sometimes I think I'm just pathetic but then other times I think, I'm not a tank.'

'Cannonfodder,' observes Frances.

'It's all right if you're the sort who can manage on four hours,' says Sally. 'Churchill. Thatcher. Bugger.'

Ben, having tipped his chair to the point of no return, carries on down towards the floor in slow motion. Frances dives in and with quiet skill prevents infant skull from hitting lino-clad concrete.

'Reflexes,' says Sally gratefully. 'Shot to pieces.'

She clasps the shaken child to her coat with absent fervour. He is drawing breath for a blare of delayed shock when the arrival of the toast deflects him.

'The camel's back,' says Sally obscurely.

'Not funny,' comments Frances, who understands that she is referring to sleep, or its absence.

Ben takes the buttery knife from the side of his plate and waves it in the air, then drops it onto his mother's coat sleeve. From there it falls to her lap and then, noisily, to the floor. She dabs at the butter stains with a tissue and bangs her forehead as she reaches beneath the table for the knife. Ben laughs and sandpapers his chin with a square of toast.

This woman Sally has a drinker's face, but her lustreless grey skin and saurian eye come not from alcohol but from prolonged lack of sleep.

As a former research student it has often occurred to her that a medical or sociology post-graduate might profitably study the phenomenon in society of a large number of professional women in their thirties suffering from exhaustion. Her third child, this bouncing boy, has woken at least four times a night since he was born. Most mornings he won't go back to sleep after five, so she has him in with her jumping and playing and singing. She hasn't shared a bedroom with her husband for eighteen months now. She'd carried on full-time through the first and second. They slept. Luck of the draw. Yes of course she has talked to her health visitor about this, she has taken the boy to a sleep clinic, she has rung Cry-sis and listened to unseen mothers in the same foundering boat. The health visitor booked her into a sleep counselling course which involved her taking an afternoon every week off work, driving an hour's round trip on the North Circular, only to listen to some well-meaning woman tell her what damage this sleep pattern was causing to the family unit, to her health, to her marriage, to the boy's less demanding siblings. Well she knew all that anyway, didn't she? After the third session she said, what's the point? Not every problem has a solution, she decided, and here it is obviously a brutally simple question of survival, of whether she cracks before he starts sleeping through. It's years now.

THESE THOUGHTS FLASH through her mind, vivid and open, but must remain unspoken as Ben's presence precludes anything much in the way of communication beyond blinking in Morse. The few words she has exchanged with this woman Frances, known only by sight after all from the nursery school queue, are the merest tips of icebergs. Such thoughts are dangerous to articulate anyway, bringing up into the air what has been submerged. Nearly all faces close in censorship at the merest hint of such talk. Put up and shut up is the rule, except with fellow mothers. Even then it can be taken as letting the side down. She yawns uncontrollably so that her eyes water, leaving her with the face of a bloodhound.

Put up and shut up is the rule, except with fellow mothers

From her handbag this tired woman Sally takes a pad and felt tips and places them in front of her son Ben, who is rolling his eyes and braying like a donkey.

'Shush, Ben,' she says. 'You're not a donkey.'

He looks at her with beautiful affectless eyes. He sucks in air and starts up a series of guttural snorts.

'You're not a piggy, Ben, stop it,' says Sally.

'Piggy,' says Ben, laughing with lunatic fervour.

'They were brilliant at work, they bent over backwards,' says Sally, rapidly, anyway. 'It was me that resigned, I thought it wasn't fair on them. I was going into work for a rest. Ben!'

'That's hard,' says Frances, watching as Sally straightens the boy in his chair and tries to engage him in colouring a picture of a rabbit in police uniform.

'Do you work then?' asks Sally, filling in one long furry ear with pink.

'Yes. No,' says Frances. 'I shouldn't be here! You know, round the edges at the moment. I mean, I must. I have. Always. Unthinkable! But, erm. You know. Freelance at the moment.'

Ben pushes the paper away from him and grasps at a handful of felt tips. He throws them against the window and cheers at the clatter they make on impact.

'No, Ben!' growls Sally through clenched teeth. 'Naughty.'

The two women grovel under the table picking up pens. Ben throws a few more after them.

WHAT FRANCES WOULD *have said had there been a quiet patch of more than five seconds was that she had worked full-time all through the babyhood of her first child, Emma, and also until her second, Rose, was three, as well as running the domestic circus, functioning as the beating heart of the family while deferring to the demands of her partner's job in that it was always her rather than him who took a day off sick when one of the girls sprained a wrist or starred in a concert, and her too of course who was responsible for finding, organising and paying for childcare and for the necessary expenditure of count- less megavolts of the vicarious emotional and practical energy involved in having someone else look after your babies while you are outside the house all day, all the deeply unrestful habits of vigilance masquerading as 'every confidence' in the girl who would, perfectly reasonably, really rather be an aerobics instructor working on Legs Tums 'n Bums.*

Then there was one childcare-based strappado too many; and she cracked. After all those years. She had come home unexpectedly in the afternoon to find the girl fast asleep on the sofa, clubbed out as she later put it, while Emma and Rose played on the stairs with needles and matches or some such. Could be worse, her sensible woman-in-the-workplace voice said; she's young, she likes a good time and why shouldn't she; nothing happened, did it? To hell with that, her mother-in-the- house voice said; I could be the one on the sofa rather than out there busting a gut and barely breaking even.

She needed work, she loved work, she was educated for it. Didn't she, Sally, feel the same way? She'd never asked her

partner for money; no, they were equals, pulling together. Well,
work was fabulous while you were there, it was what you had
to do before and after work that was the killer. It was good for
the girls to see their mother out working in the real world, he
said when she talked of feeling torn apart; a role model. There's
no need to feel guilty, he would begin, *with God-like compas-*
sion. It's not guilt, you fool. It's the unwelcome awareness that
being daily ripped in half is not good, not even ultimately. I
agree with all the reasons. 'I'm sorry, they've got to realise that
you are a person in your own right and have work to do.' I
couldn't agree more. 'Women have always worked, except for
that brief sinister time in the fifties.' Yes. *But had they always*
had to work a ten-hour day at a full hour's commuting distance
from their babies while not showing by a murmur or a flicker
what this was doing to them?

So here she was after all these years 'gone freelance', that coy
phrase, cramming a full-time job into their school hours and
also the evenings once they'd gone to bed. She had a large enve-
lope of sweets pinned to the wall by the telephone so that she
could receive work calls to the noise of lollipop-sucking rather
than shrilling and howls. And now, of course, she had no sick
pay, paid holiday, pension or maternity leave should she be so
foolish as to find herself pregnant again. Just as the Welfare
State she'd been raised to lean on was packing up.

UNFORTUNATELY NOT ONE word of this makes it into the
light of day, as Ben is creating.

'It was more fun at work,' Frances bursts out, watching

Sally wipe the child's buttery jawline with another of the inexhaustible supply of tissues from her bag. 'You get some *respect* at work.'

'My last childminder,' says Sally. She flinches.

'Snap,' says Frances.

The two women sip their powerless cappuccinos.

'In a couple of years' time, when this one starts school,' says Sally, 'I could probably get back, get by with an au pair in term-time. Someone to collect them from school, get their tea. But then there's the holidays.'

'Very long, the holidays,' agrees Frances.

'Not fair on the poor girl,' says Sally. 'Not when she doesn't speak English. Now if it was just Leo he'd be fine,' she continues, off on another tack, thinking aloud about her two eldest children. 'But Gemma is different.'

The child Ben slides off his chair and runs over to the glass-fronted display of sandwich fillings, the metal trays of damp cheese, dead ham and tired old tuna mixed with sweetcorn kernels. He starts to hit the glass with the flat of his hand. There is a collective intake of breath and everyone turns to stare. As she lurches over to apologise and expostulate, Sally's mind continues to follow her train of thought, silently addressing Frances even if all that Frances can see of her is a bumbling, clucking blur.

CHILDREN ARE ALL *different, Sally thinks on, and they are different from birth. Her own son Leo has a robust nature, a level temperament and the valuable ability to amuse himself, which is what makes him so easy to care for. He has smilingly greeted more than half a dozen childminders in his time, and waved them goodbye with equal cheeriness. Gemma, however, was born more anxious, less spirited. She cries easily and when her mother used to leave for work would abandon herself to despair. She is crushingly jealous of this youngest child Ben. She wants to sit on Sally's lap all the time when she is there, and nags and whines like a neglected wife, and clings so hard that all around are uncomfortably filled with irritation. She has formed fervid attachments to the aforementioned childminders, and has wept bitterly at their various departures. Well, Gemma may thrive better now her mother is at home, or she may not; the same could be said of her mother. Time will tell, but by then of course it will be then and not now, and Sally will be unemployable whichever way it has turned out.*

'OOF,' GRUNTS SALLY, returning with her son, who leaps within her arms like a young dolphin. She sits him firmly on his chair again.

'My neighbour's au pair wrote their car off last week,' says Frances. 'Nobody hurt, luckily.'

They both shudder.

'We're so lucky,' they agree, po-faced, glum, gazing at zany Ben as he stabs holes into the police rabbit with a sharp red pen. Sally yawns uncontrollably, then Frances starts up where she leaves off.

After all, they're getting nowhere fast.

An elderly woman pauses as she edges past their table on the way to the till. She cocks her head on one side and smiles brightly at Ben, whose mouth drops open. He stares at her, transfixed, with the expression of a seraph who has understood the mystery of the sixth pair of wings. His mother Sally knows that he is in fact temporarily dumbstruck by the woman's tremendous wart, which sits at the corner of her mouth with several black hairs sprouting from it.

'What a handsome little fellow,' says the woman fondly. 'Make the most of it, dear,' she continues, smiling at Sally. 'It goes so fast.' Sally tenses as she smiles brightly back, willing her son not to produce one of his devastating monosyllables. Surely he does not know the word for wart yet.

'Such a short time,' repeats the woman, damp-eyed.

WELL, NOT REALLY, *thinks Frances. Sometimes it takes an hour to go a hundred yards. Now she knows what she knows she puts it at three and a half years per child, the time spent exhausted, absorbed, used up; and, what's more, if not, then something's wrong. That's a whole decade if you have three! This is accurate, wouldn't you agree, she wants to ask Sally; this is surely true for all but those women with Olympic physical stamina, cast-iron immune systems, steel-clad nerves and sensitivities. Extraordinary women; heroines, in fact. But what about the strugglers? The ordinary mother strugglers? Why do they educate us, Sally, only to make it so hard for us to work afterwards? Why don't they insist on hysterectomies for girls who want further education and have done with it? Of course none of this will get said. There is simply no airspace.*

BEN'S EYES HAVE sharpened and focused on his admirer's huge side-of-the-mouth wart.

'Witch,' he says, loud and distinct.

'Ben,' says Sally. She looks ready to cry, and so does the older woman, who smiles with a hurt face and says, 'Don't worry, dear, he didn't mean anything,' and moves off.

'WITCH,' shouts Ben, following her with his eyes.

At this point, Sally and Frances give up. With a scraping of chairs and a flailing of coats, they wordlessly heave themselves and Ben and his paraphernalia up to the counter, and pay, and go. They won't try that again in a hurry. They smile briefly at each other as they say goodbye, wry and guarded. They have exchanged little more than two hundred words inside this hour, and how much friendship can you base on that?

After all, it's important to put up a decent apologia for your life; well, it is to other people, mostly; to come up with a convincing defence, to argue your corner. It's nothing but healthy, the way the sanguine mind does leap around looking for the advantages of any new shift in situation. And if you can't, or won't, you will be shunned. You will appear to be a whiner, or a malcontent. Frances knows this, and so does Sally.

Even so they pause and turn and give each other a brief, gruff, foolish hug, with the child safely sandwiched between them.

Hey Yeah Right Get a Life

DORRIE STOOD AT THE EDGE of the early-morning garden and inhaled a column of chilly air. After the mulch of soft sheets and stumbling down through the domestic rubble and crumbs and sleeping bodies, it made her gasp with delight, outside, the rough half-light of March and its menthol coldness.

The only other creature apart from herself was next door's cat which sauntered the length of the fence's top edge stately as a *fin de siècle* roué returning from a night of pleasure. That was what she was after, the old feline assurance that she had a place here. Of course you couldn't expect to remain inviolate; but surely there had to be some part of yourself you could call your own without causing trouble. It couldn't *all* be spoken for. She watched the cat hunch its shoulders and soundlessly pour itself from the fence onto the path.

Nowadays those few who continued to see Dorrie at all registered her as a gloomy, timid woman who had grown rather fat and over-protective of her three infants. They sighed with impatient pity to observe how easily small anxieties took possession of her, how her sense of proportion appeared to have receded along with her horizons. She was never still, she was always available, a conciliatory twittering fusspot. Since the arrival of the children, one, two and then three, in the space of four years, she had broken herself into little pieces like a biscuit and was now scattered all over the place. The urge – indeed, the necessity – to give everything, to throw herself on the bonfire, had been shocking; but now it was starting to wear off.

Back in the warmth of her side of the bed she lay listening to Max's breathing, and the clink and wheezing protest of a milk float, then the first front doors slamming as the trainee accountants and solicitors set off for the station. There was a light pattering across the carpet and a small round figure stood by the bed. She could see the gleam of his eyes and teeth smiling conspiratorially in the blanching dark.

'Come on then,' she whispered. 'Don't wake Daddy.'

He climbed into bed and curled into her, his head on her shoulder, his face a few inches from hers, gazed into her eyes and heaved a happy sigh. They lay looking at each other, breathing in each other's sleepy scent; his eyes were guileless, unguarded and intent, and he gave a little occasional beatific smile.

'Where's your pyjama top?' she whispered.

'Took it *off*,' he whispered back. 'Too itchy.'

Since the arrival of the children she had broken herself into little pieces like a biscuit and was now scattered all over the place

'It's *not* itchy,' she tutted. 'I'll put some special oil in your bath tonight.'

His chest was like a huge warm baroque pearl. She satined the side of her face against it for a moment.

'When are you going to stop wearing nappies at night?' she scolded in a whisper.

'When I'm four,' he chuckled, and shifted his pumpkin padding squarely onto her lap.

Max stirred and muttered something.

'Ssssh,' said Robin, placing a forefinger against his mother's lips and widening his eyes for emphasis.

They watched Max's dark bearded face break into a yawn, a seadog or a seagod about to rally his crew. He was waking up. Robin wriggled under the bedclothes to hide. Last night it had been her under the bedclothes and Max's hands on her head while she brought him off with her mouth. Then she had curled into him, her head on his shoulder, until he fell into a dense sleep, and she basked like a lioness in the sun. Next, gently unwinding herself from his knotty embrace she had glided along to the next room and plucked this heavy boy from his bed, standing him, sleep-dazed, in front of the lavatory, pointing the shrimp of his penis for him, whispering encouragement as the water hissed, before closing in on him with the midnight nappy.

Max's eyes flickered awake and he smiled at Dorrie.

'Mmmm,' he said. 'Come here.' He reached over and grabbed her, buried his face in her neck, and then as he reached downwards his hands encountered his son.

'No! No!' screeched Robin, laughing hectically. 'Get *away*, Daddy!'

This brought his siblings, Martin and Maxine, running from their bedroom and they hurled themselves into the heap of bodies. Max struggled out of it growling, and was gone.

The three children shoved and biffed their way into shares of her supine body. Robin clung to his central stake, arms round her neck, head between her breasts, kicking out at attempts to supplant him. Martin hooked his legs round her waist and lay under her left arm gnawing his nails and complaining it wasn't fair. Maxine burrowed at her right side, all elbows and knees, until she settled in the crook of her other arm, her head beside Dorrie's on the pillow.

'Mummy. A good heart is never proud. Is that true?' said Maxine.

'What?'

'It was on my *Little Mermaid* tape. I can make my eyes squelch, listen.'

'Oof, careful, Robin,' said Dorrie, as Robin brought his head up under her chin and crashed her teeth together.

'Goodbye,' said Max from the doorway.

'Don't forget we're going out tonight,' said Dorrie from the pillows.

'Oh yes,' said Max. He looked at the heap of bodies on the bed. 'Your mother and I were married eight years ago today,' he said into the air, piously.

'Where was *I*?' said Maxine.

'*Not* going out,' hissed Robin, gripping Dorrie more tightly. 'Stay inner house, Mummy.'

'And I'm not going to stand for any nonsense like that,' growled Max. He glared at his youngest son. 'Get off your mother, she can't move. It's ridiculous.'

'It's all right, Max,' said Dorrie. 'Don't make yourself late.'

'Go away, Daddy,' shouted Robin.

'Yeah,' joined in Martin and Maxine. 'Go away, Daddy.'

Max glared at them impotently, then turned on his heel like a pantomime villain. A moment later they heard the front door slam.

'Yesss!' said Robin, punching the air with his dimpled fist. The bed heaved with cheers and chuckles.

'You shouldn't talk to Daddy like that,' said Dorrie.

'Horble Daddy,' said Robin dismissively.

'He's not horble,' huffed Dorrie. 'Horrible. Time to get up.'

They all squealed and clutched her harder, staking her down with sharp elbows and knees wherever they could.

'You're hurting me,' complained Dorrie. 'Come on, it really is time to get up.' And at last she extracted herself like a slow giantess from the cluster of children, gently detaching their fingers from her limbs and nightdress.

When she turned back from drawing the curtains, Martin was painting his shins with a stick of deodorant while Maxine sat on the floor, galloping her round bare heels in the cups of a discarded bra, pulling on the straps like a jockey, with shouts of 'Ya! Ya! Giddy up, boy!' Robin ran round and round his mother's legs, wrapping and rewrapping her nightdress. Then he rolled on the carpet with both hands round her ankle, a lively leg-iron, singing alleluia, alleluia, alleluia.

'Don't do that, Martin,' said Dorrie as she climbed into yesterday's jeans and sweatshirt. But he was already on to something else, crossing the floor with a bow-legged rocking gait, a pillow across his shoulders, groaning under its imaginary weight and bulk.

'I'm Robin Hood carrying a deer,' he grinned back over his shoulder. Maxine roared with laughter, hearty as a Tudor despot.

'Come on, darlings,' Dorrie expostulated feebly. 'Help me get you dressed.'

They ran around her and across the landing, ignoring her, screeching, singing, bellowing insults and roaring into the stairwell. She pulled vests and socks and jumpers from various drawers, stepping around them like a slave during a palace orgy. Their separate energies whizzed through the air, colliding constantly, as random as the weather. She grabbed Martin as he shot past and started to strip off his nightclothes.

'No!' he yelled and tore himself free, running off trouserless. He was as quick as she was slow. It was like wading through mud after dragonflies.

'I hate you!' he was screaming at Maxine now for some reason. 'I wish you were dead!'

'Now now,' said Dorrie. 'That's not very nice, is it.'

Then there were pinches and thumps and full-chested bellows of rage. By the time she had herded them down for the cornflakes stage, they had lived through as many variants of passion as occur in the average Shakespeare play. She looked at their momentarily woebegone faces streaked with tears of fury over whichever was the most recent hair-pulling or jealousy or bruising, she had lost track, and said with deliberate cheer, 'Goodness, if we could save all the tears from getting ready in the mornings, if we could collect them in a bucket, I could use them to do the washing up.'

All three faces broke into wreathed smiles and appreciative laughter at this sally, and then the row started up again. They did not take turns to talk, but cut across each other's words with reckless thoughtlessness. She was trying to think through the hairbrushing, shoe-hunting, tooth-cleaning, packed lunch for Martin, empty toilet roll cylinder for Maxine's Miss Atkinson, with an eye on the clock, but it was a non-starter.

'SHUSH,' she shouted. 'I can't hear myself THINK.'

'Are you thinking?' asked Maxine curiously.

'No,' she said. 'Hurry UP.'

It was not in fact possible to think under these conditions; no train of thought could ever quite leave the platform, let alone arrive at any sort of destination. This was what the mothers at the school gates meant when they said they were brain-dead, when they told the joke about the secret of childcare being a frontal lobotomy or a bottle in front of me. This was why she had started waking in the small hours, she realised, even though heaven knew she was tired enough without that, even though she was still being woken once or twice a night by one or the other of them; not Max because he had to be fresh for work and anyway they wouldn't want him. They wanted *her*. But when they were all safe, breathing regularly, asleep, quiet, she was able at last to wait for herself to grow still, to grow still and alive so that the sediment settled and things grew clearer. So that she could *think*.

'Mrs Piper said Jonathan had nits and she sent him home,' said Martin, lifting his face up. She was brushing his hair, and pushed his brow back down against her breastbone. Then, more muffled, came, '*Don't* make me look like Elvis de Presto.'

'What I want to know, Mum,' he said as she pushed him back and knelt at Maxine's feet to struggle with her shoe buckles. 'What I *need* to know, nobody will tell me,' he continued crossly, 'is, is God there, *can* he hold the whole world in his hand – or is he like the Borrowers? I mean, what is he? Is he a man? Is he a cow?'

She was working grimly against the clock now. Her hands shook. She was shot to hell. Maxine was complaining of a blister on her little toe. Dorrie ran off upstairs like a heifer for the plaster roll and cut a strip and carefully fitted it round the pea-sized top joint of the toe. Maxine moaned and screamed, tears squirted from her eyes, her face became a mask of grief as she felt the plaster arrangement inside her sock even more uncomfortable once strapped into her shoe. It all had to be removed again and a square quarter inch of plaster carefully applied like a miniature postage stamp to the reddened area.

'We're late,' hissed Dorrie, but even in the middle of this felt a great sick thud of relief that it was not two years ago when she had been racing against the clock to get to work pretending to them there that all this had not just happened. When at last she had caved in, when she had given in her notice, it felt like giving up the world, the flesh and the devil. It had been terrible at first, the loss of breadth, the loss of adult company. There were the minutes at various school gates with the other mothers, but you couldn't really call that proper talk, not with all the babies and toddlers on at them. After all she had not managed to keep both worlds up in the air. She knew she had failed.

She picked Robin up and jammed him into the buggy.

'Teeth!' said Martin, baring his own at her. 'You've forgotten about teeth!'

'Never mind,' she said through hers, gritted, manoeuvring the buggy across the front doorstep. 'Come on.'

'Why?' asked Martin, pulling his school jumper up to his eyes and goggling at himself in front of the hall mirror. 'Burglars don't show their noses, Mum. Look. Mum.'

THESE DAYS MARTIN flew off towards the playground as soon as they reached the school gate, for which she was profoundly grateful. For his first five years he had been full of complaints, fault-finding and irritability. He still flew into towering rages and hit her and screamed until he was pink or blue in the face, often several times a day. As he was her first child this had come as a shock. She even asked the doctor about it, and the doctor had smiled and said his sounded a fiery little nature but he would no doubt learn to control himself in time. 'Also, all behaviour is *learned* behaviour,' said the doctor reprovingly. 'Never shout back or you'll just encourage him.' Plenty of the other mothers had children who behaved similarly, she noticed after a while. You just had to take it, and wait for time to pass. It could take years. It did. He was loud, waspish, frequently agitated and a constant prey to boredom. When she saw him nibbling his nails, tired and white as a cross elf, she would draw him onto her lap and make a basket of her arms around him. She saw his lack of ease in the world, and grieved for him, and knew it was her fault because she was his mother.

Maxine was less irritable but more manipulative. Her memory was terrifyingly precise and long – yesterday, for example, she had raged at Dorrie for stealing a fruit pastille, having remembered the colour of the top one from several hours before. She relished experiments and emotional mayhem. Her new trick this week was to fix you with her pale pretty eye, and say, quite coolly, 'I hate you.' This poleaxed Dorrie. And yet this little girl was also utterly unglazed against experience, as fresh and easily hurt as one of those new daffodil shoots.

Only when Robin was born had she realised what it was to have what is commonly known as an easy child. No rhyme nor reason to it. Same treatment, completely different. They were as they were as soon as they were born, utterly different from each other. That was something at least. It couldn't *all* be her fault.

Now it was halfway through Martin's first school year and he had settled in well. It was wonderful. She glanced in passing at other less fortunate mothers talking low and urgent with their infants, entwined and unlinking, like lovers, bargaining with furtive tears, sobs, clinging arms, angry rejections, pettishness and red eyes.

It was the same when she dropped Maxine off at nursery school half an hour later. On the way out she and Robin passed a little girl of three or so saying to her mother, 'But Mummy, I *miss* you'; and the mother, smartly dressed, a briefcase by her, rather tightly reasoning with her, murmuring, glancing at her watch. Dorrie felt herself break into a light sympathetic sweat.

The little scene brought back Robin's trial morning there last week. He had refused to walk through the nursery school's entrance and was shouting and struggling as she carried him in. She had set him down by a low table of jigsaw puzzles and told him sternly that she would sit over there in that corner for five minutes, that his sister was just over there in the Wendy house, and that he must let her go quietly. From the toy kitchen he had brought her a plastic cupcake with a fat ingratiating smile.

'Here y'are,' he'd said.

'Save it for when I come to pick you up,' Dorrie had said, handing it back to him, pity and coldness battling through her like warring blood corpuscles. At last he had given her a resigned kiss on the cheek and gone off to the painting table without another look. (Two hours alone, for the first time in months. Wait till he's at school, said the mothers; you won't know yourself.) She dashed a tear away, sneering at her own babyishness.

Now, today, there was this precious time with Robin. He liked to be around her, within a few yards of her, to keep her in his sight, but he did not pull the stuffing out of her as the other two did. He did not demand her thoughts and full attention like Maxine; nor that she should identify and change colour like litmus paper with his every modulation of emotion as it occurred, which was what Martin seemed to need. Sometimes those two were so extravagantly exacting, they levied such a fantastic rate of slavish fealty that they left her gasping for air.

No, Robin talked to his allies and foes, *sotto voce*, in the subterranean fields which ran alongside the privet-hedged landscape in which they moved together. He sent out smiles or little waves while Dorrie was working, and took breaks for a hug or to pause and drink squash, him on her lap like a stalwart beanbag.

She sorted the dirty whites from the coloured wash up on the landing, and he put them into the washing basket for her. Up and down the stairs she went with round baskets of washing, the smell of feet and bottoms, five sets, fresh and smelly, all different. Robin stuffed the garments into the washing machine one by one, shutting the door smartly and saying 'There!' and smiling with satisfaction. She did some handwashing at the sink, and he pushed a chair over across the floor to stand on, and squeezed the garments, then took handfuls of the soap bubbles that wouldn't drain away and trotted to and from the bucket on the mat with them.

'What a helpful boy you are!' she said. He beamed.

'Now I'm going to iron some things including Daddy's shirt for tonight,' she said. 'So you must sit over there because the iron is dangerous.'

'Hot,' he agreed, with a sharp camp intake of breath.

He sat down on the floor with some toys in a corner of the kitchen and as she ironed she looked over now and then at his soft thoughtfully frowning face as he tried to put a brick into a toy car, the curve of his big soft cheek like a mushroom somehow, and his lovely close-to-the-head small ears. He gave an unconscious sigh of concentration; his frequent sighs came right from deep in the diaphragm. Squab or chub or dab had been the words which best expressed him until recently, but now he was growing taller and fining down, his limbs had lost their chubbiness and his body had become his own.

No longer could she kiss his eyelids whenever she wished, nor pretend to bite his fingers, nor even stroke his hair with impunity. He was a child now, not a baby, and must be accorded his own dignity. The baby was gone, almost.

Abruptly she put the iron on its heel and swooped down on him, scooped him up and buried her nose in his neck with throaty growling noises. He huffed and shouted and laughed as they swayed struggling by the vegetable rack. She tickled him and they sank down to the lino laughing and shouting, then he rubbed his barely there velvet nose against hers like an Eskimo, his eyes close and dark and merry, inches from hers, gazing in without shame or constraint.

It was going to be a long series of leave-takings from now on, she thought; goodbye and goodbye and goodbye; that had been the case with the others, and now this boy was three and a half. Unless she had another. But then Max would leave. Or so he said. This treacherous brainless greed for more of the same, it would finish her off if she wasn't careful. If she wasn't already.

She took Max's shirt upstairs on a hanger and put the rest of the ironing away. What would she wear tonight? She looked at her side of the wardrobe. Everything that wasn't made of T-shirt or sweatshirt fabric was too tight for her now. Unenthusiastically she took down an old red shirt-dress, looser than the rest, and held it up against her reflection in the full-length mirror. She used to know what she looked like, she used to be interested. Now she barely recognised herself. She peeled off her sweatshirt and jeans and pulled the dress on. She looked enormous. The dress was straining at the seams. She looked away fast, round the bedroom, the unmade bed like a dog basket, the mess everywhere, the shelves of books on the wall loaded with forbidden fruit, impossible to broach, sealed off by the laws of necessity from her maternal eyes. During the past five years, reading a book had become for her an activity engaged in at somebody else's expense.

The doorbell rang and she answered it dressed as she was. Robin hid behind her.

'Gemma's got to be a crocodile tomorrow,' said Sally, who lived two roads away. 'We're desperate for green tights, I've tried Mothercare and Boots and then I thought of Maxine. I don't suppose?'

'Sorry,' said Dorrie. 'Only red or blue.'

'Worth a try,' said Sally, hopeless. 'You look dressed up.'

'I look fat,' said Dorrie. 'Wedding anniversary,' she added tersely.

'Ah,' said Sally. 'How many years?'

'Eight,' said Dorrie. 'Bronze. Sally, can you remember that feeling before all the family stuff kicked in, I know it's marvellous but. You know, that spark, that feeling of fun and – and lightness, somehow.'

Immediately Sally replied, 'It's still there in me but I don't know for how much longer.'

'You could try Verity,' said Dorrie. 'I seem to remember she put Hannah in green tights last winter to go with that holly berry outfit.'

'So she did!' said Sally. 'I'll give her a ring.'

'Kill,' whispered Robin, edging past the women into the

tiny front garden; 'Die, megazord,' and he crushed a snail shell beneath his shoe. Half hidden beneath the windowsill he crouched in a hero's cave. Across the dangerous river of the front path he had to save his mother, who was chatting to a wicked witch. He started round the grape hyacinths as though they were on fire and squeezed his way along behind the lilac bush, past cobwebs and worms, until he burst out fiercely into the space behind the hedge. She was being forced to walk the plank. He leaped into the ocean and cantered sternly across the waves.

THEY WERE LATE coming out of nursery school, and Dorrie stood with the other mothers and au pairs in the queue. Some were chatting, some were sagging and gazing into the middle distance.

In front of her, two women were discussing a third just out of earshot.

'Look at her nails,' said the one directly in front of Dorrie. 'You can always tell. Painted fingernails mean a rubbish mother.'

'I sometimes put nail polish on if I'm going out in the evening,' said the other.

'*If*,' scoffed the first. 'Once in a blue moon. And then you make a mess of it, I bet. You lose your touch. Anyway, you've got better things to do with your time, you give your time to your children, not to primping yourself up.'

Robin pushed his head between Dorrie's knees and clutched her thighs, a mini Atlas supporting the world.

Dorrie saw it was Patricia from Hawthornden Avenue.

'*I* was thinking of doing my nails today,' said Dorrie.

'What on earth *for*?' laughed Patricia. She was broad in the beam, clever but narrow-minded.

'Wedding anniversary,' said Dorrie. 'Out for a meal.'

'There you are then,' said Patricia triumphantly, as though she had proved some point.

'I had a blazing row with *my* husband last night,' said Patricia's friend. 'And I was just saying to myself, Right that's it, I was dusting myself down ready for the off, when I thought, No, hang on a minute, I *can't* go. I've got three little children, I've *got* to stay.'

Patricia's eyebrows were out of sight, she reeled from side to side laughing. They all laughed, looking sideways at each other, uneasy.

'Have you noticed what happens now that everyone's splitting up,' snorted Patricia's friend. 'I've got friends, their divorce comes through and do you know they say it's amazing! They lose weight and take up smoking and have all the weekends to themselves to do *whatever they want* in because the men take the children off out then.'

'Divorce,' said Dorrie ruminatively. 'Yes. You get to thirty-seven, married, three kids, and you look in the mirror, at least I did this morning, and you realise – it's a shock – you realise nothing else is supposed to happen until you die. Or you spoil the pattern.'

The nursery school doors opened at last. Dorrie held her arms out and Maxine ran into them. Maxine had woken screaming at five that morning, clutching her ear, but then the pain had stopped and she had gone back to sleep again. Dorrie had not. That was when she had gone downstairs and into the garden.

'The doctor's going to fit us in after her morning surgery, so I must run,' said Dorrie, scooping Maxine up to kiss her, strapping Robin into the buggy.

'Mum,' called Maxine, as they galloped slowly along the pavement, 'Mum, Gemma says I must only play with her or she won't be my friend. But I told her Suzanne was my best friend. Gemma's only second best.'

'Yes,' said Dorrie. 'Mind that old lady coming towards us.'

'Suzanne and me really wanted Gemma to play Sour Lemons but Shoshaya wanted her to play rabbits,' panted Maxine. 'Then Shoshaya cried and she told Miss Atkinson. And Miss Atkinson told us to let her play. But Gemma wanted to play Sour Lemons with me and Suzanne and she did.'

'Yes,' said Dorrie. She must get some milk, and extra cheese for lunch. She ought to pick up Max's jacket from the cleaners. Had she got the ticket? Had she got enough cash? Then there was Max's mother's birthday present to be bought and packed up and posted off to Salcombe, and a card. She had to be thinking of other people all the time or the whole thing fell apart. It was like being bitten all over by soldier ants without being able to work up enough interest to deal with them. Sometimes she found herself holding her breath for no reason at all.

'Why do you always say yes?' said Maxine.

'What?' said Dorrie. They stood at the kerb waiting to cross. She looked up at the top deck of the bus passing on the other side and saw a young man sitting alone up there. He happened to meet her eye for a moment as she stood with the children, and the way he looked at her, through her, as though she were a greengrocer's display or a parked car, made her feel less than useless. She was a rock or stone or tree. She was nothing.

'Why do you always say yes?' said Maxine.

'What?' said Dorrie.

'Why do you always say YES!' screamed Maxine in a rage.

'Cross *now*,' said Dorrie, grabbing her arm and hauling her howling across the road as she pushed the buggy.

They turned the corner into the road where the surgery was and saw a small boy running towards them trip and go flying, smack down onto the pavement.

'Oof,' said Maxine and Robin simultaneously.

The child held up his grazed hands in grief and started to split the air with his screams. His mother came lumbering up with an angry face.

'I told you, didn't I? I told you! You see? God was looking down and he saw you were getting out of control. You wouldn't do what I said, would you. And God said, *right*, and He made you fall down like that and that's what happens when you're like that. So now maybe you'll listen the next time!'

Dorrie looked away, blinking. That was another thing, it

had turned her completely soft. The boy's mother yanked him up by the arm, and dragged him past, moralising greedily over his sobs.

'She should have hugged him, Mummy, shouldn't she,' said Maxine astutely.

'Yes,' said Dorrie, stopping to blow her nose.

THE TATTERED COVERS of the waiting room magazines smiled over at them in a congregation of female brightness and intimacy. The women I see in the course of a day, thought Dorrie, and it's women only (except Max at the end of the day), we can't really exchange more than a sentence or two of any interest because of our children. At this age they need us all the time; and anyway we often have little in common except femaleness and being in the same boat. Why should we? She scanned the lead lines while Robin and Maxine chose a book from the scruffy pile – 'How to dump him: twenty ways that work'; 'Your hair: what does it say about you?', 'Countdown to your best orgasm'. Those were the magazines for the under-thirties, the free-standing feisty girls who had not yet crossed the ego line. And of course some girls never did cross the ego line. Like men, they stayed the stars of their own lives. Then there was this lot, this lot here with words like juggle and struggle across their covers, these were for her and her like – 'Modern motherhood: how do you measure up?'; 'Is your husband getting enough: time management and you'; 'Doormat etiquette: are you too nice?'

Am I too *nice*? thought Dorrie. They even took *that* away. Nice here meant weak and feeble, *she* knew what it meant. Nice was now an insult, whereas self had been the dirty word when she was growing up. For girls, anyway. She had been trained to think of her mother and not be a nuisance. She couldn't remember ever saying (let alone being asked) what she wanted. To the point of thinking she didn't really mind what she wanted as long as other people were happy. It wasn't long ago.

The doctor inspected Maxine's eardrum with her pointed torch, and offered a choice.

'You can leave it and hope it goes away. That's what they'd do on the Continent.'

'But then it might flare up in the night and burst the eardrum. That happened to Martin. Blood on the pillow. Two sets of grommets since then.'

'Well, *tant pis*, they'd say. They're tough on the Continent. Or it's the usual amoxcyllin.'

'I don't like to keep giving them that. But perhaps I could have some in case it gets very painful later. And not give it otherwise.'

'That's what I'd do,' said the doctor, scribbling out a prescription.

'How are you finding it, being back at work?' asked Dorrie timidly but with great interest. The doctor had just returned after her second baby and second five-month maternity leave.

'Fine, fine,' smiled the doctor, rubbing her eyes briefly,

tired blue eyes kind in her worn face. 'In fact of course it's easier. I mean, it's hard in terms of organisation, hours, being at full stretch. But it's still easier than being at home. With tiny children you really have to be so . . . selfless.'

'Yes,' said Dorrie, encouraged. 'It gets to be a habit. In the end you really do lose yourself. Lost. But then they start to be not tiny.'

'Lost!' said Maxine. 'Who's lost? What you talking about, Mum? *Who's* lost?'

The doctor glanced involuntarily at her watch.

'I'm sorry,' said Dorrie, bustling the children over to the door.

'Not at all,' said the doctor. She did look tired. 'Look after yourself.'

Look after yourself, thought Dorrie as she walked the children home, holding her daughter's hand as she skipped and pulled at her. She glanced down at her hand holding Maxine's, plastic shopping bags of vegetables over her wrist, and her nails looked uneven, not very clean. According to the nursery school queue, that meant she was a good mother. She did nothing for herself. She was a vanity-free zone. Broken nails against that tight red dress wouldn't be very alluring, but all that was quite beyond her now. By schooling herself to harmlessness, constant usefulness to others, she had become a big fat zero.

By the time they got home Dorrie was carrying Robin straddled African-style across her front, and he was alternately sagging down protesting, then straightening his back and climbing her like a tree. He had rebelled against the buggy, so she had folded it and trailed it behind her, but when he walked one of his shoes hurt him; she knew the big toenail needed cutting but whenever his feet were approached he set up a herd-of-elephants roar. She made a mental note to creep up with the scissors while he slept. I can't see how the family would work if I let myself start wanting things again, thought Dorrie; give me an inch and I'd run a mile, that's what I'm afraid of.

INDOORS, SHE PEELED vegetables while they squabbled and played around her legs. She wiped the surfaces while answering long strings of zany questions which led up a spiral staircase into the wild blue nowhere.

'I know when you're having a thought, Mummy,' said Maxine. 'Because when I start to say something then you close your eyes.'

'Can I have my Superman suit?' said Robin.

'In a minute,' said Dorrie, who was tying up a plastic sack of rubbish.

'Not in a minute,' said Robin. '*Now*.'

The thing about small children was that they needed things all day long. They wanted games set up and tears wiped away and a thousand small attentions. This was all fine until you started to do something else round them, or something that wasn't just a basic menial chore, she thought, dragging the hoover out after burrowing in the stacking boxes for the Superman suit. You had to be infinitely elastic and adaptable; all very laudable but this had the concomitant effect of slowly but surely strangling your powers of concentration.

Then Superman needed help in blowing his nose, and next he wanted his cowboys and Indians reached down from the top of the cupboard. She forgot what she was thinking about.

Now she was chopping onions finely as thread so that Martin would not be able to distinguish their texture in the meatballs and so spit them out. (Onions were good for their immune systems, for their blood.) She added these to the minced lamb and mixed in eggs and breadcrumbs then shaped the mixture into forty tiny globes, these to bubble away in a tomato sauce, one of her half-dozen flesh-concealing ruses against Maxine's incipient vegetarianism. (She knew it was technically possible to provide enough protein for young children from beans as long as these were eaten in various careful conjunctions with other beans – all to do with amino acids – but she was not want-ing to plan and prepare even more separate meals – Max had his dinner later in the evening – not just yet anyway – or she'd be simmering and peeling till midnight.)

The whole pattern of family life hung for a vivid moment above the chopping board as a seamless cycle of nourish-ment and devoural. And after all, children were not teeth extracted from you. Perhaps it was necessary to be devoured.

Dorrie felt sick and faint as she often did at this point

in the day, so she ate a pile of tepid left-over mashed potato and some biscuits while she finished clearing up and peace-keeping. The minutes crawled by. She wanted to lie down on the lino and pass out.

Maxine's nursery school crony, Suzanne, came to play after lunch. Dorrie helped them make a shop and set up tins of food and jars of dried fruit, but they lost interest after five minutes and wanted to do colouring in with felt tips. Then they had a fight over the yellow. Then they played with the Polly Pockets, and screamed, and hit each other. Now, now, said Dorrie, patient but intensely bored, as she pulled them apart and calmed them down and cheered them up.

At last it was time to drop Suzanne off and collect Martin. Inside the school gates they joined the other mothers, many of whom Dorrie now knew by name or by their child's name, and waited at the edge of the playground for the release of their offspring.

'I can't tell you anything about Wednesday until Monday,' said Thomas' mother to a woman named Marion. A note had been sent back in each child's reading folder the previous day, announcing that the last day before half term would finish at twelve. The women who had part-time jobs now started grumbling about this, and making convoluted webs of arrangements. 'If you drop Neil off at two then my neighbour will be there, you remember, he got on with her last time all right, that business with the spacehopper; then Verity can drop Kirsty by after Tumbletots and I'll be back

with Michael and Susan just after three-thirty. Hell! It's bal-
let. Half an hour later. Are you *sure* that's all right with you?'

'They're late,' said Thomas' mother, glancing at her watch.

'So your youngest will be starting nursery after Easter,'
said Marion to Dorrie. 'You won't know yourself.'

'No,' said Dorrie. She reached down to ruffle Robin's
feathery hair; he was playing around her legs.

'Will you get a job then?' asked Marion.

'Um, I thought just for those weeks before summer I'd
get the house straight, it's only two hours in the morning.
And a half,' said Dorrie in a defensive rush. 'Collect my
thoughts. If there are any.'

'Anyway, you do your husband's paperwork in the evenings, don't you?' said Thomas' mother. 'The accounts and
that. VAT.'

'You get so you can't see the wood for the trees, don't
you,' said Dorrie. 'You get so good at fitting things round
everything else. Everybody else.'

'I used to be in accounts,' said Marion. 'B.C. But I
couldn't go back now. I've lost touch. I couldn't get into
my suits any more, I tried the other day. I couldn't do it! I'd
hardly cover the cost of the childcare. I've lost my nerve.'

'My husband says he'll back me up one hundred per
cent when the youngest starts school,' said Thomas'
mother pensively. 'Whatever job I want to do. But no way
would he be able to support change which would end by
making his working life more difficult, he said.'

'That's not really on, then, is it?' said Marion. 'Unless

you get some nursery school work to fit round school hours. Or turn into a freelance something.'

'Some people seem to manage it,' said Thomas' mother. 'Susan Gloverall.'

'I didn't know she was back at work.'

'Sort of. She's hot-desking somewhere off the A3, leaves the kids with a childminder over Tooting way. Shocking journey, but the devil drives.'

'Keith still not found anything, then? That's almost a year now.'

'I know. Dreadful really. I don't think it makes things any, you know, easier between them. And of course she can't leave the kids with him while he's looking. Though she said he's watching a lot of TV.'

'What about Nicola Beaumont, then?' said Dorrie.

'Oh her,' said Marion. 'Wall-to-wall nannies. No thank you.'

'I could never make enough to pay a nanny,' said Thomas' mother. 'I never earned that much to start with. And then you have to pay their tax on top, out of your own taxed income. You'd have to earn eighteen thousand at least before you broke even if you weren't on the fiddle. I've worked it out.'

'Nearer twenty-two these days,' said Marion. 'In London. Surely.'

'Nicola's nice though,' said Dorrie. 'Her daughter Jade, the teenage one, she's babysitting for us tonight.'

'Well she never seems to have much time for me,' said Marion.

'I think she just doesn't have much time full stop,' said Dorrie.

'Nor do any of us, dear,' said Thomas' mother. 'Not *proper* time.'

'Not time to yourself,' said Marion.

'I bet she gets more of that than I do. She commutes, doesn't she? There you are then!'

They were all laughing again when the bell went.

'HARRY SWALLOWED HIS tooth today,' said Martin. 'Mrs Tyrone said it didn't matter, it would melt inside him.' He wiggled his own front tooth, an enamel tag, tipping it forward with his fingernail. Soon there would be the growing looseness, the gradual twisting of it into a spiral, hanging on by a thread, and the final silent snap.

'He won't get any money from the Tooth Fairy, will he, Mum,' said Martin. 'Will he, Mum? Will he, Mum? Mum. Mum!'

'Yes,' said Dorrie. 'What? I expect so, dear.' She was peeling carrots and cutting them into sticks.

'And Kosenia scratched her bandage off today, and she's got eczema, and she scratched off, you know, that stuff on top, like the cheese on Shepherd's Pie, she just lifted it off,' Martin went on.

'Crust,' said Dorrie.

'Yes, crust,' said Martin. 'I'm not eating those carrots. No way.'

'Carrots are very good for you,' said Dorrie. 'And tomorrow I'm going to pack some carrot sticks in your lunch box and I want you to eat them.'

'Hey yeah right,' gabbled Martin. 'Hey yeah right get a life!'

And he marched off to where the other two were watching a story about a mouse who ate magic berries and grew as big as a lion. Television was nothing but good and hopeful and stimulating compared with the rest of life so far as she could see. Certainly it had been the high point of her own childhood. Her mother thought she spoiled her children, but then most of her friends said their mothers thought the same about them. She was trying to be more tender with them – she and her contemporaries – to offer them choices rather than just tell them what to do; to be more patient and to hug them when they cried rather than briskly talk of being brave; never to hit them. They felt, they all felt they were trying harder than their parents had ever done, to love well. And one of the side effects of this was that their children were incredibly quick to castigate any shortfall in the quality of attention paid to them.

Now they were fighting again. Martin was screaming and chattering of injustice like an angry ape. Maxine shrilled back at him with her ear-splitting screech. Robin sat on the ground, hands to his ears, sobbing deep-chested sobs of dismay.

She groaned with boredom and frustration. Really she could not afford to let them out of her sight yet; not for another six months, anyway; not in another room, even with television.

'Let's all look at pictures of Mummy and Daddy getting married,' she shouted above the din, skilfully deflecting the furies. Sniffing and shuddering they eventually allowed themselves to be gathered round the album she had dug out, while she wiped their eyes and noses and clucked mild reproaches. The thing was, it did not do simply to turn off. She was not a part of the action but her involved presence was required as it was necessary for her to be ready at any point to step in as adjudicator. What did not work was when she carried on round them, uninvolved, doing the chores, thinking her own thoughts and making placatory noises when the din grew earsplitting. Then the jaws of anarchy opened wide.

Soon they were laughing at the unfamiliar images of their parents in the trappings of romance, the bright spirited faces and trim figures.

'Was it the best day in your life?' asked Maxine.

There was me, she thought, looking at the photographs; there used to be me. She was the one who'd put on two stone; he still looked pretty fit. The whole process would have been easier, she might have been able to retain some self-respect, if at some point there had been a formal handing over like Hong Kong.

At the end of some days, by the time each child was

breathing regularly, asleep, she would stand and wait for herself to grow still, and the image was of an ancient vase, crackle-glazed, still in one piece but finely crazed all over its surface. I'm shattered, she would groan to Max on his return, hale and whole, from the outside world.

Now, AT THE end of just such a day, Dorrie was putting the children down while Max had a bath after his day at work. It was getting late. She had booked a table at L'Horizon and arranged for Jade to come round and baby-sit at eight. They had not been out together for several months, but Dorrie had not forgotten how awful it always was.

It was twenty to eight, and Robin clung to her.

'Don't go, Mummy, don't go,' he sobbed, jets of water spouting from his eyes, his mouth a square buckle of anguish.

'Don't be silly,' said Dorrie, with her arms round him. 'I've got to go and change, darling. I'll come straight back.'

'No you won't,' he bellowed. Martin watched with interest, nibbling his nails.

'He's making me feel sad, Mum,' commented Maxine. 'I feel like crying now too.'

'So do I,' said Dorrie grimly.

'What's all the noise?' demanded Max, striding into the room drubbing his hair with a towel. 'Why aren't you children asleep yet?'

Robin took a wild look at his father and, howling with

fresh strength, tightened his grip on Dorrie with arms, legs and fingers.

'Let go of your mother this minute,' snarled Max in a rage, starting to prise away the desperate fingers one by one. Robin's sobs became screams, and Maxine started to cry.

'Please, Max,' said Dorrie. 'Please don't.'

'This is ridiculous,' hissed Max, wrenching him from her body. Dorrie watched the child move across the line into hysteria, and groaned.

'Stop it, Daddy!' screamed Martin, joining in, and downstairs the doorbell rang.

'Go and answer it then!' said Max, pinning his frantic three-year-old son to the bed.

'Oh God,' said Dorrie as she stumbled downstairs to open the door to the babysitter.

'Hello, Jade!' she said with a wild fake smile. 'Come in!'

'Sounds like I'm a bit early,' said Jade, stepping into the hall, tall and slender and dressed in snowy-white shirt and jeans.

'No, no, let me show you how to work the video, that's just the noise they make on their way to sleep,' said Dorrie, feeling herself bustle around like a fat dwarf. It seemed pathetic that she should be going out and this lovely girl staying in. The same thought had crossed Jade's mind, but she had her whole life ahead of her, as everyone kept saying.

'Any problems, anything at all, if one of them wakes and

asks for me, please ring and I'll come back, it's only a few minutes away.'

'Everything'll be *fine*,' said Jade, as if to a fussy infant. 'You shouldn't worry so much.'

'I'll swing for that child,' they heard Max growl from the landing, then a thundering patter of feet, and febrile shrieks.

'EIGHT YEARS, EH,' said Max across the candlelit damask. 'My Old Dutch. No need to look so tragic.'

Dorrie was still trying to quiet her body's alarm system, the waves of miserable heat, the klaxons of distress blaring in her bloodstream from Robin's screams.

'You've got to go out sometimes,' said Max. 'It's getting ridiculous.'

'I'm sorry I didn't manage to make myself look nice,' said Dorrie. '*You* look nice. Anyway, it's four pounds an hour. It's like sitting in a taxi.'

Max was big and warm, sitting relaxed like a sportsman after the game, but his eyes were flinty.

'It's just arrogant, thinking that nobody else can look after them as well as you,' he said.

'They can't,' mumbled Dorrie, under her breath.

'You're a dreadful worrier,' said Max. 'You're always worrying.'

'Well,' said Dorrie. 'Somebody's got to.'

'Everything would carry on all right, you know, if you stopped worrying.'

'No it wouldn't. I wish it would. But it wouldn't.'

Lean and sexually luminous young waiting staff glided gracefully around them.

'Have you chosen,' he said, and while she studied the menu he appraised her worn face, free of make-up except for an unaccustomed and unflattering application of lipstick, and the flat frizz of her untended hair. She was starting to get a double chin, he reflected wrathfully; she had allowed herself to put on more weight. Here he was on his wedding anniversary sitting opposite a fat woman. And if he ever said anything, *she* said, the children. It showed a total lack of respect; for herself; for him.

'I just never seem to get any time to myself,' muttered Dorrie. She felt uneasy complaining. Once she'd stopped bringing in money she knew she'd lost the right to object. So did he.

'It's a matter of discipline,' said Max, sternly.

He felt a terrible restlessness at this time of year, particularly since his fortieth. The birthday cards had all been about being past it. Mine's a pint of Horlicks, jokes about bad backs, expanding waistlines, better in candlelight. There it stretched, all mapped out for him; a long or not-so-long march to the grave; and he was forbidden from looking to left or right. He had to hold himself woodenly impervious, it would seem, since every waking moment was supposed to be a married one. All right for her, she could stun herself with children. But he needed a romantic motive or life wasn't worth living.

He could see the food and drink and television waiting for him at each day's end, and the thickening of middle age, but he was buggered if he was going to let himself go down that route. He watched Dorrie unwisely helping herself to sautéed potatoes. Her body had become like a car to her, he thought, it got her around, it accommodated people at various intervals, but she herself seemed to have nothing to do with it any more. She just couldn't be bothered.

What had originally drawn him to her was the balance between them, a certain tranquil buoyancy she had which had gone well with his own more explosive style. These days she was not so much tranquil as stagnant, while all the buoyancy had been bounced off. He wished he could put a bomb under her. She seemed so apathetic except when she was loving the children. It made him want to boot her broad bottom whenever she meandered past him in the house, just to speed her up.

The children had taken it out of her, he had to admit. She'd had pneumonia after Maxine, her hair had fallen out in handfuls after Robin, there had been two caesareans, plus that operation to remove an ovarian cyst. The saga of her health since babies was like a seaside postcard joke, along with the mothers-in-law and the fat-wife harridans. After that childminder incident involving Martin breaking his leg at the age of two, she'd done bits of part-time but even that had fizzled out soon after Robin, so now she wasn't bringing in any money at all. When he married her, she'd had an interesting job, she'd earned a bit, she was lively and sparky; back in the mists of time. Now he had the whole pack of them on his back and he was supposed to be as philosophical about this as some old leech-gatherer.

He didn't want to hurt her, that was the trouble. He did not want the house to fly apart in weeping and wailing and children who would plead with him not to go, Daddy. He did not want to seem disloyal, either. But, he thought wildly, neither could he bear being sentenced to living death. Things were going to have to be different. She couldn't carry on malingering round the house like this. It wasn't fair. She shouldn't expect. He felt a shocking contraction of pity twist his guts. Why couldn't she bloody well look after herself better? He took a deep breath.

'Did I mention about Naomi,' he said casually, spearing a floret of broccoli.

Naomi was Max's right-hand woman at the builder's yard. She oversaw the stock, manned the till when necessary, sorted the receipts and paperwork for Dorrie to deal with at home and doled out advice about undercoats to the customers. She had been working for them for almost two years.

'Is she well?' asked Dorrie. 'I thought she was looking very white when I saw her last Wednesday.'

'Not only is she not well, she's throwing up all over the place,' said Max heavily. 'She's pregnant,' he added in a muffled voice, stuffing more vegetables into his mouth.

'Pregnant?' said Dorrie. 'Oh!' Tears came to her eyes and she turned to scrabble under the table as if for a dropped napkin. So far she had managed to hide from him her insane lusting after yet another.

'That's what I thought,' sighed Max, misinterpreting her reaction.

'I'm so pleased for her, they've been wanting a baby for ages,' said Dorrie, and this time it was her voice that was muffled.

'So of course I've had to let her go,' said Max, looking at his watch.

'You've *what*?' said Dorrie.

'It's a great shame, of course. I'll have to go through all that with someone else now, showing them the ropes and so on.'

'How *could* you, Max?'

'Look, I knew you'd be like this. I *know*. It's a shame isn't it, yes; but there it is. That's life. It's lucky it happened when it did. Another few weeks and she'd have been able to nail me to the wall, unfair dismissal, the works.'

'But they need the money,' said Dorrie, horrified. 'How are they going to manage the mortgage now?'

'He should pull his finger out then, shouldn't he,' shrugged Max. 'He's public sector anyway, they'll be all right. Look, Dorrie, I've got a wife and children to support.'

'Get her back,' said Dorrie. 'Naomi will be fine. She's not like me, she'll have the baby easily, she won't get ill afterwards, nor will the baby. We were unlucky. She's very capable, she's not soft about things like childminders. You'd be mad to lose her.'

'Actually,' said Max, 'I've offered her a part-time job when she is ready to come back, and I rather think that might suit us better too. If I keep her below a certain number of hours.'

'What did Naomi say to *that*?'

'She was still a bit peeved about being let go,' said Max. 'But she said she'd think about it. If she could combine it with another part-time job. Beggars can't be choosers. I mean, if she chooses to have a baby, that's her choice.'

'I see,' said Dorrie carefully. 'So who will take over her work at the yard meanwhile?'

'Well, you, of course,' said Max, swallowing a big forkful of chop, his eyes bulging. He hurried on. 'Robin starts at nursery after Easter, Maxine's nearly finished there, and Martin's doing fine at school full-time now. So you can work the mornings, then you can collect Robin and Maxine and bring them along for a sandwich and work round them from then till it's time to pick up Martin. We can leave the paperwork till the evening. We'll save all ways like that. He's a big boy now, he can potter around.'

'He's only three and a half,' she said breathlessly. 'And when would I do the meals and the ironing and the cleaning and the shopping in all this?'

'Fit it in round the edges,' said Max. 'Other women do. It'll be good for you, get you out of the house. Come on, Dorrie, I can't carry passengers forever. You'll have to start pulling your weight again.'

It was towards the end of the main course and they

had both drunk enough house white to be up near the surface.

'They're hard work, young children, you know,' she said.

'You said yourself they're getting easier every day. You said so yourself. It's not like when they were all at home all day screaming their heads off.'

'It is when they're on holiday,' she said. 'That's nearly twenty weeks a year, you know. What happens *then*?'

'You're off at a tangent again,' he said, sighing, then demanded, 'What *do* you want out of life?'

'It's not some sort of anaconda you've got to wrestle with,' said Dorrie. She realised that this latest sequestration of her hours would send her beside herself. Loss of inner life, that's what it was; lack of any purchase in the outside world, and loss of all respect; continuous unavoidable Lilliputian demands; numbness, apathy and biscuits. She was at the end of her rope.

'We can't just wait for things to fall into our laps though,' said Max, thinking about his own life.

'We're doing all right,' said Dorrie.

'That doesn't mean to say we couldn't do better. We need to expand.'

'We're managing the mortgage,' said Dorrie. 'I think we should be grateful.'

'That's the spirit,' said Max. 'That's the spirit that made this island great. Stand and stare, eh. Stand and stare.'

'What would you prefer?' said Dorrie. 'Life's a route march, then you die?'

'But then *you've* got what you wanted, haven't you – the children.'

'You are horrible,' said Dorrie. She took a great gulp of wine and drained her glass. 'It's about how well you've loved and how well you've been loved.' She didn't sound very convincing, she realised, in fact she sounded like Thought for the Day. She sounded like some big sheep bleating.

'I don't know what it is, Dorrie,' he said sadly. 'But you're all damped down. You've lost your spirit. You're not there any more.'

'I know. I know. But that's what I'm trying to say. You think I've just turned into a boring saint. But I'm still there. If you could just take them for a few hours now and then and be *nice* to them, if I just had a bit of quiet time . . .'

'I'm not exactly flourishing either, you know. You're getting to me.'

'Sorry. Sorry. I seem to be so dreary these days. But . . .'

'That's what I mean. Such a victim. Makes me want to kick you.'

'Don't, Max. Please don't. We've got to go back to that girl and pay her first.'

'Just being miserable and long-suffering, you think that'll make me sorry for you.'

'Max . . .'

'But it makes me hate you, if you must know.'

BACK AT THE house, Max handed Dorrie his wallet and went off upstairs. He was tired as he brushed his teeth, and angry at the way the evening had gone; nor did he like his bad-tempered reflection in the bathroom mirror. Soon he was asleep, frowning in release like a captive hero.

Dorrie meanwhile was fumbling with five-pound notes, enquiring brightly as to whether Jade had had a quiet evening.

'Oh yes, there wasn't a sound out of them once you'd gone,' said Jade, not strictly truthfully, still mesmerised by the beautiful eyes of the sex murderer with the razor on the screen. There had actually been a noise from the boys' bedroom and when she had put her head around the door sure enough the younger one was lying in a pool of sick. But he was breathing fine so she left him to it, it wasn't bothering him and no way was she going to volunteer for that sort of thing. She was getting paid to babysit, not to do stuff like that. That would have been right out of order.

'Would you like to stay and finish your video?' asked Dorrie politely, flinching as she watched the razor slit through filmstar flesh.

'No, that's all right,' said Jade reluctantly. She flicked the remote control and the bloody image disappeared. She sighed.

'Well, thank you again,' said Dorrie. 'It's lovely to know I can leave them with someone I can trust.'

'That's OK,' said Jade. 'No problem.' And with a royal yawn she made her exit.

It took Dorrie half an hour or so to bathe the dazed Robin, to wash the acrid curds holding kernels of sweet-corn and discs of peas from his feathery hair and wrap him in clean pyjamas and lay him down in the big bed beside his noble-looking father, where he fell instantly asleep, slumbering on a cloud of beauty.

She kissed his warm face and turned back, her body creaking in protest, to the job in hand. Downstairs in the midnight kitchen she scraped the duvet cover and pillow case with the knife kept specifically for this purpose, dumping the half-digested chyme into the sink, running water to clear it away, then scraping again, gazing out of the window into the blackness of the wild garden, yearning at the spatter of rain on the glass and the big free trees out there with their branches in the sky.

Their needs were what was set. Surely that was the logic of it. It was for *her* to adapt, accommodate, modify in order to allow the familial organism to flourish. Here she was weeping over her own egotism like a novice nun, for goodness sake, except it was the family instead of God. But still it was necessary, selflessness, for a while, even if it made you spat on by the world. By your husband. By your children. By yourself.

She wanted to smash the kitchen window. She wanted to hurt herself. Her ghost was out there in the garden, the ghost from her free-standing past. If she kept up this business of reunion, it would catch hold of her hands and saw her wrists to and fro across the jagged glass. It would tear her from the bosom of this family she had breastfed. No. She must stay this side of the glass from now on, thickening and cooling like some old planet until at last she killed the demands of that self-regarding girl out there.

She twisted and squeezed water from the bedlinen she had just rinsed. If she were to let herself be angry about this obliteration, of her particular mind, of her own relish for things, then it would devour the family. Instead she must let it gnaw at her entrails like some resident tiger. This was not sanctimony speaking but necessity. All this she knew but could not explain. She was wringing the sheet with such force that it creaked.

'Fresh air,' she said aloud, and tried to open the window in front of her. It was locked, clamped tight with one of the antiburglar fastenings which they had fitted on all the windows last summer. She felt around in the cupboard above the refrigerator for the key, but it wasn't in its usual place. She hunted through the rows of mugs, the tins of tuna and tomatoes, the bags of rice and flour and pasta, and found it at last inside the glass measuring jug.

Leaning across the sink she unlocked the window and opened it onto the night. A spray of rain fell across her face and she gasped. There was the cold fresh smell of wet earth. It occurred to her that this might not necessarily be killer pain she was feeling, not terrible goodbyeforever pain as she had assumed; and she felt light-headed with the shock of relief.

Perhaps this was not the pain of wrist-cutting after all.

Instead, the thought came to her, it might be the start of that intense outlandish sensation that comes after protracted sleep; the feeling in a limb that has gone numb, when blood starts to flow again, sluggishly at first, reviving; until after a long dormant while that limb is teeming again, tingling into life.

Out in the garden, out in the cold black air, she could see the big trees waving their wild bud-bearing branches at her.

Heavy Weather

'YOU SHOULD NEVER HAVE MARRIED ME.'

'I haven't regretted it for an instant.'

'Not *you*, you fool! *Me!* You shouldn't have got me to marry you if you loved me. Why *did* you, when you knew it would let me in for all *this*. It's not *fair!*'

'I didn't know. I know it's not. But what can I do about it?'

'I'm being mashed up and eaten alive.'

'I know. I'm sorry.'

'It's not your fault. But what can I do?'

'I don't know.'

So the conversation had gone last night in bed, followed by platonic embraces. They were on ice at the moment, so far as anything further was concerned. The smoothness and sweet smell of their children, the baby's densely packed pearly limbs, the freshness of the little girl's breath when she yawned, these combined to accentuate the grossness of their own bodies. They eyed each other's mooching adult bulk with mutual lack of enthusiasm, and fell asleep.

At four in the morning, the baby was punching and shouting in his Moses basket. Frances forced herself awake, lying for the first moments like a flattened boxer in the ring trying to rise while the count was made. She got up and fell over, got up again and scooped Matthew from the basket. He was huffing with eagerness, and scrabbled crazily at her breasts like a drowning man until she lay down with him. A few seconds more and he had abandoned himself to rhythmic gulping. She stroked his soft head and drifted off. When she woke again, it was six o'clock and he was sleeping between her and Jonathan.

For once, nobody was touching her. Like Holland she lay, aware of a heavy ocean at her seawall, its weight poised to race across the low country.

The baby was now three months old, and she had not had more than half an hour alone in the twenty-four since his birth in February. He was big and hungry and needed her there constantly on tap. Also, his two-year-old sister Lorna was, unwillingly, murderously jealous, which made everything much more difficult. This time round was harder, too, because when one was asleep the other would be awake and vice versa. If only she could get them to nap at the same time, Frances started fretting, then she might be able to sleep for some minutes during the day and that would get her through. But they wouldn't, and she couldn't. She had taken to muttering I can't bear it, I can't bear it, without realising she was doing so until she heard Lorna chanting I can't bear it! I can't bear it! as she skipped along beside the pram, and this made her blush with shame at her own weediness.

Now they were all four in Dorset for a week's holiday. The thought of having to organise all the food, sheets, milk, baths and nappies made her want to vomit.

In her next chunk of sleep came that recent nightmare, where men with knives and scissors advanced on the felled trunk which was her body.

'How would you like it?' she said to Jonathan. 'It's like a doctor saying, now we're just going to snip your scrotum in half, but don't worry, it mends very well down there, we'll stitch you up and you'll be fine.'

It was gone seven by now, and Lorna was leaning on the bars of her cot like Farmer Giles, sucking her thumb in a ruminative pipe-smoking way. The room stank like a lion house. She beamed as her mother came in, and lifted her arms up. Frances hoisted her into the bath, stripped her down and detached the dense brown nappy from between her knees. Lorna carolled, 'I can sing a *rain*bow,' raising her faint fine eyebrows at the high note, graceful and perfect, as her mother sluiced her down with jugs of water.

'WHY DOES EVERYTHING take so *long*?' moaned Jonathan. 'It only takes *me* five minutes to get ready.'

Frances did not bother to answer. She was sagging with

the effortful boredom of assembling the paraphernalia needed for a morning out in the car. Juice. Beaker with screw-on lid. Flannels. Towels. Changes of clothes in case of car sickness. Nappies. Rattle. Clean muslins to catch Matthew's curdy regurgitations. There was more. What was it?

'Oh, come on, Jonathan, think,' she said. 'I'm fed up with having to plan it all.'

'What do you think I've been doing for the last hour?' he shouted. 'Who was it that changed Matthew's nappy just now? Eh?'

'Congratulations,' she said. 'Don't shout or I'll cry.'

Lorna burst into tears.

'Why is everywhere always such a *mess*,' said Jonathan, picking up plastic spiders, dinosaurs, telephones, beads and bears, his grim scowl over the mound of primary colours like a traitor's head on a platter of fruit.

'I *want* dat spider, Daddy!' screamed Lorna. 'Give it to me!'

During the ensuing struggle, Frances pondered her tiredness. Her muscles twitched as though they had been tenderised with a steak bat. There was a bar of iron in the back of her neck, and she felt unpleasantly weightless in the cranium, a gin-drinking side effect without the previous fun. The year following the arrival of the first baby had gone in pure astonishment at the loss of freedom, but second time round it was spinning away in exhaustion. Matthew woke at one a.m. and four a.m., and Lorna at

six-thirty a.m. During the days, fatigue came at her in concentrated doses, like a series of time bombs.

'Are we ready at last?' said Jonathan, breathing heavily.
'Are we ready to go?'

'Um, nearly,' said Frances. 'Matthew's making noises. I
think I'd better feed him, or else I'll end up doing it in a
lay-by.'

'Right,' said Jonathan. 'Right.'

Frances picked up the baby. 'What a nice fat parcel
you are,' she murmured in his delighted ear. 'Come on, my
love.'

'Matthew's not your love,' said Lorna. '*I'm* your love.
You say, C'mon love, to *me*.'

'You're *both* my loves,' said Frances.

The baby was shaking with eagerness, and pouted his
mouth as she pulled her shirt up. The little girl sat down
beside her, pulled up her own teeshirt and applied a teddy
bear to her nipple. She grinned at her mother.

Frances looked down at Matthew's head, which was
shaped like a brick or a small wholemeal loaf, and remembered again how it had come down through the middle of
her. She was trying very hard to lose her awareness of this
fact, but it would keep re-presenting itself.

'D'you know,' said Lorna, free hand held palm upwards,
hyphen eyebrows lifting, 'd'you know, I was sucking my
thumb when I was coming downstairs, mum, mum, then
my foot slipped and my thumb came out of my mouth.'

'Well, that's very interesting, Lorna,' said Frances.

Two minutes later, Lorna caught the baby's head a ring-ing smack and ran off. Jonathan watched as Frances lunged clumsily after her, the baby jouncing at her breast, her stained and crumpled shirt undone, her hair a bird's nest, her face craggy with fatigue, and found himself dubbing the tableau, Portrait of rural squalor in the manner of William Hogarth. He bent to put on his shoes, stuck his right foot in first then pulled it out as though bitten.

'What's *that*,' he said in tones of profound disgust. He held his shoe in front of Frances' face.

'It looks like baby sick,' she said. 'Don't look at me. It's not my fault.'

'It's all so bloody *basic*,' said Jonathan, breathing hard, hopping off towards the kitchen.

'If you think that's basic, try being me,' muttered Frances. 'You don't know what basic *means*.'

'Daddy put his foot in Matthew's sick,' commented Lorna, laughing heartily.

AT CERNE ABBAS they stood and stared across at the chalky white outline of the Iron-Age giant cut into the green hill.

'It's enormous, isn't it,' said Frances.

'Do you remember when we went to stand on it?' said Jonathan. 'On that holiday in Child Okeford five years ago?'

'Of course,' said Frances. She saw the ghosts of their frisky former selves running around the giant's limbs and up onto his phallus. Nostalgia filled her eyes and stabbed her smartly in the guts.

'The woman riding high above with bright hair flapping free,' quoted Jonathan. 'Will you be able to grow *your* hair again?'

'Yes, yes. Don't look at me like that, though. I know I look like hell.'

A month before this boy was born, Frances had had her hair cut short. Her head had looked like a pea on a drum. It still did. With each pregnancy, her looks had hurtled five years on. She had started using sentences beginning, 'When I was young.' Ah, youth! Idleness! Sleep! How pleasant it had been to play the centre of her own stage. And how disorientating was this overnight demotion from Brünnhilde to spear-carrier.

'What's that,' said Lorna. 'That *thing*.'

'It's a giant,' said Frances.

'Like in Jacknabeanstork?'

'Yes.'

'But what's that *thing*. That thing on the giant.'

'It's the giant's thing.'

'Is it his stick thing?'

'Yes.'

'My baby budder's got a stick thing.'

'Yes.'

'But I haven't got a stick thing.'

'No.'

'Daddy's got a stick thing.'

'Yes.'

'But *Mummy* hasn't got a stick thing. We're the same, Mummy.'

She beamed and put her warm paw in Frances'.

'YOU CAN'T SEE round without an appointment,' said the keeper of Hardy's cottage. 'You should have telephoned.'

'We did,' bluffed Jonathan. 'There was no answer.'

'When was that?'

'Twenty to ten this morning.'

'Hmph. I was over sorting out some trouble at Clouds Hill. T. E. Lawrence's place. All right, you can go through. But keep them under control, won't you.'

They moved slowly through the low-ceilinged rooms, whispering to impress the importance of good behaviour on Lorna.

'This is the room where he was born,' said Jonathan, at the head of the stairs.

'Do you remember from when we visited last time?' said Frances slowly. 'It's coming back to me. He was his mother's first child, she nearly died in labour, then the doctor thought the baby was dead and threw him into a basket while he looked after the mother. But the midwife noticed he was breathing.'

'Then he carried on till he was eighty-seven,' said Jonathan.

They clattered across the old chestnut floorboards, on into another little bedroom with deep thick-walled windowseats.

'Which one's your favourite now?' asked Frances.

'Oh, still *Jude the Obscure*, I think,' said Jonathan. 'The tragedy of unfulfilled aims. Same for anyone first generation at university.'

'Poor Jude, laid low by pregnancy,' said Frances. 'Another victim of biology as destiny.'

'Don't *talk*, you two,' said Lorna.

'At least Sue and Jude aimed for friendship as well as all the other stuff,' said Jonathan.

'Unfortunately, all the other stuff made friendship impossible, didn't it,' said Frances.

'Don't *talk*!' shouted Lorna.

'Don't shout!' said Jonathan. Lorna fixed him with a calculating blue eye and produced an ear-splitting scream. The baby jerked in his arms and started to howl.

'Hardy didn't have children, did he,' said Jonathan above the din. 'I'll take them outside, I've seen enough. You stay up here a bit longer if you want to.'

Frances stood alone in the luxury of the empty room and shuddered. She moved around the furniture and thought fond savage thoughts of silence in the cloisters of a convent, a blessed place where all was monochrome and non-viscous. Sidling up unprepared to a mirror on the wall she gave a yelp at her reflection. The skin was the colour and texture of pumice stone, the grim jaw set like a lion's muzzle. And the eyes, the eyes far back in the skull were those of a herring three days dead.

Jonathan was sitting with the baby on his lap by a row of lupins and marigolds, reading to Lorna from a newly acquired guide book.

'When Thomas was a little boy he knelt down one day in a field and began eating grass to see what it was like to be a sheep.'

'What did the sheep say?' asked Lorna.

'The sheep said, er, so now you know.'

'And what else?'

'Nothing else.'

'Why?'

'What do you mean, why?'

'Why?'

'Look,' he said when he saw Frances. 'I've bought a copy of *Jude the Obscure* too, so we can read to each other when we've got a spare moment.'

'Spare moment!' said Frances. 'But how lovely you look with the children at your knees, the roses round the cottage door. How I would like to be the one coming back from work to find you all bathed and brushed, and a hot meal in the oven and me unwinding with a glass of beer in a hard-earned crusty glow of righteousness.'

'I don't get that,' Jonathan reminded her.

'That's because I can't do it properly yet,' said Frances. 'But, still, I wish it could be the other way round. Or at least, half and half. And I was thinking, what a cheesy business Eng. Lit. is, all those old men peddling us lies about life and love. They never get as far as this bit, do they.'

'Thomas 1840, Mary 1842, Henry 1851, Kate 1856,' read Jonathan. 'Perhaps we could have two more.'

'I'd kill myself,' said Frances.

'What's the matter with you?' said Jonathan to Matthew, who was grizzling and struggling in his arms.

'I think I'll have to feed him again,' said Frances.

'What, already?'

'It's nearly two hours.'

'Hey, you can't do that here,' said the custodian, appearing at their bench like a bad fairy. 'We have visitors from all over the world here. Particularly from Japan. The Japanese are a very modest people. And they don't come all this way to see THAT sort of thing.'

'It's a perfectly natural function,' said Jonathan.

'So's going to the lavatory!' said the custodian.

'Is it all right if I take him over behind those hollyhocks?' asked Frances. 'Nobody could possibly see me there. It's just, in this heat he won't feed if I try to do it in the car.'

The custodian snorted and stumped back to his lair.

Above the thatched roof the huge and gentle trees rustled hundreds of years' worth of leaves in the pre-storm stir. Frances shrugged, heaved Matthew up so that his socks dangled on her hastily covered breast, and retreated to the hollyhock screen. As he fed, she observed the green-tinged light in the garden, the crouching cat over in a bed of limp snapdragons, and registered the way things look before an onslaught, defenceless and excited, tense and passive. She thought of Bathsheba Everdene at bay, crouching in the bed of ferns.

When would she be able to read a book again? In life before the children, she had read books on the bus, in the bathroom, in bed, while eating, through television, under radio noise, in cafés. Now, if she picked one up, Lorna shouted, 'Stop reading, Mummy,' and pulled her by the nose until she was looking into her small cross face.

Jonathan meandered among the flowerbeds flicking through *Jude the Obscure*, Lorna snapping and shouting at his heels. He was ignoring her, and Frances could see he had already bought a tantrum since Lorna was now entered into one of the stretches of the day when her self-control flagged and fled. She sighed like Cassandra but didn't have the energy to nag as he came towards her.

'Listen to this,' Jonathan said, reading from *Jude the Obscure*. '"Time and circumstance, which enlarge the views of most men, narrow the views of women almost invariably."'

'Is it any bloody wonder,' said Frances.

'I want you to *play* with me, Daddy,' whined Lorna.

'Bit of a sexist remark, though, eh?' said Jonathan.

'Bit of a sexist process, you twit,' said Frances.

Lorna gave Matthew a tug which almost had him on the ground. Torn from his milky trance, he quavered, horror-struck, for a moment, then, as Frances braced herself, squared his mouth and started to bellow.

Jonathan seized Lorna, who became as rigid as a steel girder, and swung her high up above his head. The air was split with screams.

'Give her to me,' mouthed Frances across the awe-inspiring noise.

'She's a noise terrorist,' shouted Jonathan.

'Oh, please let me have her,' said Frances.

'You shouldn't give in to her,' said po-faced Jonathan, handing over the flailing parcel of limbs.

'Lorna, sweetheart, look at me,' said Frances.

'Naaoow!' screamed Lorna.

'Shshush,' said Frances. 'Tell me what's the matter.'

Lorna poured out a flood of incomprehensible complaint, raving like a chimpanzee. At one point, Frances deciphered, 'You always feed MATTHEW.'

'You should *love* your baby brother,' interposed Jonathan.

'You can't tell her she *ought* to love anybody,' snapped Frances. 'You can tell her she must behave properly, but you can't tell her what to feel. Look, Lorna,' she continued, exercising her favourite distraction technique. 'The old man is coming back. He's cross with us. Let's run away.'

Lorna turned her streaming eyes and nose in the direction of the custodian, who was indeed hotfooting it across the lawn towards them, and tugged her mother's hand.

The two of them lurched off, Frances buttoning herself up as she went.

THEY FOUND THEMSELVES corralled into a cement area at the back of the Smuggler's Arms, a separate space where young family pariahs like themselves could bicker over fish fingers. Waiting at the bar, Jonathan observed the comfortable tables inside, with their noisy laughing groups of the energetic elderly tucking into plates of gammon and plaice and profiteroles.

'Just look at them,' said the crumpled man beside him, who was paying for a trayload of Fanta and baked beans. 'Skipped the war. Nil unemployment, home in time for tea.' He took a great gulp of lager. 'Left us to scream in our prams, screwed us up good and proper. When our kids come along, what happens? You don't see the grandparents for dust, that's what happens. They're all off out enjoying themselves, kicking the prams out the way with their Hush Puppies, spending the money like there's no tomorrow.'

Jonathan grunted uneasily. He still could not get used to the way he found himself involved in intricate conversations with complete strangers, incisive, frank, frequently desperate, whenever he was out with Frances and the children. It used to be only women who talked like that, but now, among parents of young children, it seemed to have spread across the board.

Frances was trying to allow the baby to finish his recent

interrupted feed as discreetly as she could, while watching Lorna move inquisitively among the various family groups. She saw her go up to a haggard woman changing a nappy beside a trough of geraniums.

'Your baby's got a stick thing like my baby budder.' Lorna's piercing voice soared above the babble. 'I haven't got a stick thing cos I'm a little gel. My mummy's got fur on her potim.'

Frances abandoned their table and made her way over to the geranium trough.

'Sorry if she's been getting in your way,' she said to the woman.

'Chatty, isn't she,' commented the woman unenthusiastically. 'How many have you got?'

'Two. I'm shattered.'

'The third's the killer.'

'That's my baby budder,' said Lorna, pointing at Matthew.

'He's a big boy,' said the woman. 'What did he weigh when he came out?'

'Ten pounds.'

'Just like a turkey,' she said, disgustingly, and added, 'Mine were whoppers too. They all had to be cut out of me, one way or the other.'

BY THE TIME they returned to the cottage, the air was weighing on them like blankets. Each little room was an envelope of pressure. Jonathan watched Frances collapse into a chair with children all over her. Before babies, they had been well matched. Then, with the arrival of their first child, it had been a case of Woman Overboard. He'd watched, ineffectual but sympathetic, trying to keep her cheerful as she clung on to the edge of the raft, holding out weevil-free biscuits for her to nibble, and all the time she gazed at him with appalled eyes. Just as they had grown used to this state, difficult but tenable, and were even managing to start hauling her on board again an inch at a time, just as she had her elbows up on the raft and they were congratulating themselves with a kiss, well, along came the second baby in a great slap of a wave that drove her off the raft altogether. Now she was out there in the sea while he bobbed up and down, forlorn but more or less dry, and watched her face between its two satellites dwindling to the size of a fist, then to a plum, and at last to a mere speck of plankton. He dismissed it from his mind.

'I'll see if I can get the shopping before the rain starts,' he said, dashing out to the car again, knee-deep in cow parsley.

'You really should keep an eye on how much bread we've got left,' he called earnestly as he unlocked the car. 'It won't be *my* fault if I'm struck by lightning.'

There was the crumpling noise of thunder, and silver cracked the sky. Frances stood in the doorway holding the baby, while Lorna clawed and clamoured at her to be held in her free arm.

'Oh, Lorna,' said Frances, hit by a wave of bone-aching

fatigue. 'You're too heavy, my sweet.' She closed the cottage door as Lorna started to scream, and stood looking down at her with something like fear. She saw a miniature fee-fi-fo-fum creature working its way through a pack of adults, chewing them up and spitting their bones out.

'Come into the back room, Lorna, and I'll read you a book while I feed Matthew.'

'I don't want to.'

'Why don't you want to?'

'I just don't want to.'

'Can't you tell me why?'

'Do you know, I just don't WANT to!'

'All right, *dear*. I'll feed him on my own then.'

'NO!' screamed Lorna. 'PUT HIM IN DA BIN! HE'S RUBBISH!'

'Don't scream, you little beast,' said Frances hopelessly, while the baby squared his mouth and joined in the noise.

Lorna turned the volume up and waited for her to crack. Frances walked off to the kitchen with the baby and quickly closed the door. Lorna gave a howl of rage from the other side and started to smash at it with fists and toys. Children were petal-skinned ogres, Frances realised, callous and whimsical, holding autocratic sway over lower, larger vassals like herself.

There followed a punishing stint of ricochet work, where Frances let the baby cry while she comforted Lorna; let Lorna shriek while she soothed the baby; put Lorna down for her nap and was called back three times before she gave up and let her follow her destructively around; bathed the baby after he had sprayed himself, Lorna and the bathroom with urine during the nappy-changing process; sat on the closed lavatory seat and fed the baby while Lorna chattered in the bath which she had demanded in the wake of the baby's bath.

She stared at Lorna's slim silver body, exquisite in the water, graceful as a Renaissance statuette.

'Shall we see if you'd like a little nap after your bath?' she suggested hopelessly, for only if Lorna rested would she be able to rest, and then only if Matthew was asleep or at least not ready for a feed.

'No,' said Lorna, off-hand but firm.

'Oh thank God,' said Frances as she heard the car door slam outside. Jonathan was back. It was like the arrival of the cavalry. She wrapped Lorna in a towel and they scrambled downstairs. Jonathan stood puffing on the doormat. Outside was a mid-afternoon twilight, the rain as thick as turf and drenching so that it seemed to leave no room for air between its stalks.

'You're wet, Daddy,' said Lorna, fascinated.

'There were lumps of ice coming down like tennis balls,' he marvelled.

'Here, have this towel,' said Frances, and Lorna span off naked as a sprite from its folds to dance among the chairs and tables while thunder crashed in the sky with the cumbersomeness of heavy furniture falling down uncarpeted stairs.

'*S'il vous plaît,*' said Frances to Jonathan. '*Dansez, jouez avec le petit diable, cette fille. Il faut que je* get Matthew down for a nap, she just wouldn't let me. *Je suis tellement* shattered.'

'Mummymummymummy,' Lorna chanted as she caught some inkling of this, but Jonathan threw the towel over her and they started to play ghosts.

'MY LITTLE FAT boy,' she whispered at last, squeezing his strong thighs. '*Hey*, fatty boomboom, *sweet* sugar dumpling. It's not fair, is it? I'm never alone with you. You're getting the rough end of the stick just now, aren't you.'

She punctuated this speech with growling kisses, and his hands and feet waved like warm pink roses. She sat him up and stroked the fine duck tail of hair on his baby bull neck. Whenever she tried to fix his essence, he wriggled off into mixed metaphor. And so she clapped his cloud cheeks and revelled in his nest of smiles; she blew raspberries into the crease of his neck and onto his astounded hardening stomach, forcing lion-deep chuckles from him.

She was dismayed at how she had to treat him like some sort of fancy man to spare her daughter's feelings, affecting nonchalance when Lorna was around. She would fall on him for a quick mad embrace if the little girl left the room for a moment, only to spring apart guiltily at the sound of the returning Start-rites.

The serrated teeth of remorse bit into her. In late pregnancy she had been so sandbagged that she had had barely

**And so she clapped
his cloud cheeks
and revelled in his
nest of smiles**

enough energy to crawl through the day, let alone reciprocate Lorna's incandescent two-year-old passion.

'She thought I'd come back to her as before once the baby arrived,' she said aloud. 'But I haven't.'

The baby was making the wrangling noise which led to unconsciousness. Then he fell asleep like a door closing. She carried him carefully to his basket, a limp solid parcel against her bosom, the lashes long and wet on his cheeks, lower lip out in a soft semicircle. She put him down and he lay, limbs thrown wide, spatchcocked.

AFTER THE HOLIDAY, Jonathan would be back at the office with his broad quiet desk and filter coffee while she, she would have to submit to a fate worse than death, drudging round the flat to Lorna's screams and the baby's regurgitations and her own sore eyes and body aching to the throb of next door's Heavy Metal.

The trouble with prolonged sleep deprivation was that it produced the same coarsening side effects as alcoholism. She was rotten with self-pity, swarming with irritability and despair.

When she heard Jonathan's step on the stairs, she realised that he must have coaxed Lorna to sleep at last. She looked forward to his face, but when he came into the room and she opened her mouth to speak, all that came out were toads and vipers.

'I'm smashed up,' she said. 'I'm never alone. The baby guzzles me and Lorna eats me up. I can't ever go out because I've always got to be there for the children, but you flit in and out like a humming bird. You need me to be always there, to peck at and pull at and answer the door. I even have to feed the cat.'

'I take them out for a walk on Sunday afternoons,' he protested.

'But it's like a favour, and it's only a couple of hours, and I can't use the time to read, I always have to change the sheets or make a meatloaf.'

'For pity's sake. I'm tired too.'

'Sorry,' she muttered. 'Sorry. Sorry. But I don't feel like me any more. I've turned into some sort of oven.'

They lay on the bed and held each other.

'Did you know what Hardy called *Jude the Obscure* to begin with?' he whispered in her ear. '*The Simpletons*. And the Bishop of Wakefield burnt it on a bonfire when it was published.'

'You've been reading!' said Frances accusingly. '*When* did you read!'

'I just pulled in by the side of the road for five minutes. Only for five minutes. It's such a good book. I'd completely forgotten that Jude had three children.'

'*Three?*' said Frances. 'Are you sure?'

'Don't you remember Jude's little boy who comes back from Australia?' said Jonathan. 'Don't you remember little Father Time?'

'Yes,' said Frances. 'Something very nasty happens to him, doesn't it?'

She took the book and flicked through until she reached the page where little Time and his siblings are discovered by their mother hanging from a hook inside a cupboard door, the note at their feet reading, 'Done because we are too menny.'

'What a wicked old man Hardy was!' she said, incredulous. 'How *dare* he!' She started to cry.

'You're too close to them,' murmured Jonathan. 'You should cut off from them a bit.'

'How *can* I?' sniffed Frances. '*Somebody*'s got to be devoted to them. And it's not going to be you because you know I'll do it for you.'

'They're yours, though, aren't they, because of that,' said Jonathan. 'They'll love you best.'

'They're *not* mine. They belong to themselves. But I'm not allowed to belong to *my* self any more.'

'It's not easy for me either.'

'I know it isn't, sweetheart. But at least you're still allowed to be your own man.'

They fell on each other's necks and mingled maudlin tears.

'It's so awful,' sniffed Frances. 'We may never have another.'

They fell asleep.

WHEN THEY WOKE, the landscape was quite different. Not only had the rain stopped, but it had rinsed the air free of oppression. Drops of water hung like lively glass on every leaf and blade. On their way down to the beach, the path was hedged with wet hawthorn, the fiercely spiked branches glittering with green-white flowers.

The late sun was surprisingly strong. It turned the distant moving strokes of the waves to gold bars, and dried salt patterns onto the semi-precious stones which littered the shore. As Frances unbuckled Lorna's sandals, she pointed out to her translucent pieces of chrysoprase and rose quartz in amongst the more ordinary egg-shaped pebbles. Then she kicked off her own shoes and walked wincingly to the water's edge. The sea was casting lacy white shawls onto the stones, and drawing them back with a sigh.

She looked behind her and saw Lorna building a pile of pebbles while Jonathan made the baby more comfortable in his pushchair. A little way ahead was a dinghy, and she could see the flickering gold veins on its white shell thrown up by the sun through moving seawater, and the man standing in it stripped to the waist. She walked towards it, then past it, and as she walked on, she looked out to sea and was aware of her eyeballs making internal adjustments to the new distance which was being demanded of them, as though they had forgotten how to focus on a long view. She felt an excited bubble of pleasure expanding her ribcage, so that she had to take little sighs of breath, warm and fresh and salted, and prevent herself from laughing aloud.

After some while she reached the far end of the beach.

Slowly she wheeled, like a hero on the cusp of anagnorisis, narrowing her eyes to make out the little group round the pushchair. Of course it was satisfying and delightful to see Jonathan – she supposed it *was* Jonathan? – lying with the fat mild baby on his stomach while their slender elf of a daughter skipped around him. It was part of it. But not the point of it. The concentrated delight was there to start with. She had not needed babies and their pleased-to-be-aliveness to tell her this.

She started to walk back, this time higher up the beach in the shade of cliffs which held prehistoric snails and traces of dinosaur. I've done it, she thought, and I'm still alive. She took her time, dawdling with deliberate pleasure, as though she were carrying a full glass of milk and might not spill a drop.

'I thought you'd done a Sergeant Troy,' said Jonathan. 'Disappeared out to sea and abandoned us.'

'Would I do a thing like that,' she said, and kissed him lightly beside his mouth.

Matthew reached up from his arms and tugged her hair.

'When I saw you over there by the rock pools you looked just as you used to,' said Jonathan. 'Just the same girl.'

'I am not just as I was, however,' said Frances. 'I am no longer the same girl.'

The sky, which had been growing more dramatic by the minute, was now a florid stagey empyrean, the sea a soundless blaze beneath it. Frances glanced at the baby, and saw how the sun made an electric fleece of the down on his head. She touched it lightly with the flat of her hand as though it might burn her.

'Isn't it mind-boggling,' said Jonathan. 'Isn't it impossible to take in that when we were last on this beach, these two were thin air. Or less. They're so solid now that I almost can't believe there was a time before them, and it's only been a couple of years.'

'What?' said Lorna. '*What* did you say?'

'Daddy was just commenting on the mystery of human existence,' said Frances, scooping her up and letting her perch on her hip. She felt the internal chassis, her skeleton and musculature, adjust to the extra weight with practised efficiency. To think, she marvelled routinely, to think that this great heavy child grew in the centre of my body. But the surprise of the idea had started to grow blunt, worn down by its own regular self-contemplation.

'Look, Lorna,' she said. 'Do you see how the sun is making our faces orange?'

In the flood of flame-coloured light their flesh turned to coral.

Early One Morning

SOMETIMES THEY WERE QUIET IN the car and sometimes they talked.

'Mum.'

'Yes?'

'Can I swear one time in the day? If I don't swear in the others?'

'Why?'

'In the morning. When you come and wake me. Can I say, "Bollocks"?'

'No.'

He's the only person in the world who listens to me and does what I tell him, thought Zoe. That morning when she had gone to wake him he had groaned, unconscious, spontaneous – 'Already?' Then he had reached up from his pillow to put strong sleepy arms round her neck.

For these years of her life she was spending more time alone with her boy, side by side in the car, than with anybody else, certainly far more than with her husband, thirty times more, unless you counted the hours asleep. There was the daily business of showing herself to him and to no one else; thinking aloud, urging each other on in the hunt for swimming things, car keys, maths books; yawning like cats, as they had to leave soon after seven if they were going to get to school on time. Then they might tell each other the remains of a dream during the first twenty-five minutes on the way to Freda's house, or they might sit in comfortable silence, or sometimes they would talk.

This morning when she had pointed out the sun rising in the east to hit the windscreen and blind them with its flood of flashy light, her nine-year-old boy had scoffed at her and said the earth twizzled on its axis and went round the sun, and how she, his mother, was as bad as the ancient Egyptians, how they sacrificed someone to Ra if the sun went in and finished off everybody when there was an eclipse. It's running out, this hidden time (thought Zoe). You're on your own at eleven, goes the current unwritten transport protocol, but until then you need a minder. Less than two years to go.

'I remember when I was at school,' she'd said that morning while they waited for the Caedmon Hill lights. 'It seemed to go on forever. Time goes by slowly at school. Slowly. Slowly. Then, after you're about thirty, it goes faster and faster.'

'Why?' asked George.

'I don't know,' she said. 'Maybe it's because after that you somehow know that there'll be a moment for you when there isn't any more.'

'Ooh-ah!'

Then he looked at a passing cyclist and commented, 'Big arse.'

'George!' she said, shocked.

'It just slipped out,' he said, apologetic, adult. 'You know, like when that man in the white van wouldn't let you in and you said, "Bastard."'

SOMETIMES THIS DAILY struggle and inching along through filthy air thick with the thwarted rage of ten thousand drivers gave her, Zoe, pause. It took forty-five minutes to travel the two and three-quarter miles to George's school (Sacred Heart thanks to his father's faith springing anew, rather than Hereward the Wake half a mile along), and forty-five minutes for her to come back alone in the empty car. In the afternoons it was the same, but the other way round of course, setting off a little after two-thirty and arriving back well after four. There was no train. To do the journey by bus, they would have had to catch a 63A then change and wait for a 119 at Sollers Junction. They had tried this, and it had doubled the journey time. Why couldn't there be school buses for everyone as there were in America, the mothers asked each other. Nobody knew why not, but apparently there couldn't. They were just about able to walk it in the same time as it took in the car, and they had tried this too, carrying rucksacks of homework and packed lunch and sports equipment through the soup of fumes pumped out by crawling cars. Add wind and rain, and the whole idea of pavement travel looked positively quixotic.

'I'll get it, Mum,' said George, as her mobile beeped its receipt of a text.

It was from her friend Amy, whose husband had recently left her for one of his students.

– If I say anything, he gets very angry (Amy had told her on their last phone call); he doesn't allow me to be angry.

– But he was the one to leave you.

– Yes. But now he's furious with me, he hates me.

– Do you still love him?

– I don't recognise him. I can't believe this man I ate with and slept beside for fifteen years is capable of being so cold and so, yes, cruel.

Is it true, then, that women can take grief as grief (thought Zoe), but men refuse to do that, they have to convert it into diesel in order to deal with it, all the loss and pain converted into rage?

Her husband had looked around and said, Why don't you do like Sally and Chitra and Mo, organise an au pair, pay for a few driving lessons if necessary, hand it over to someone who'll be glad of the job. She, Zoe, had thought about this, but she'd already been through it all once before, with Joe and Theresa, who were both now at secondary school. She'd done the sums, gone through the interviews in her imagination, considered the no-claims bonus; she'd counted the years for which her work time would be cut in half, she'd set off the loss of potential income against the cost of childcare, and she'd bitten the bullet. 'It's your choice,' said Patrick. And it was.

'You're a loser, Mum,' her daughter Theresa had told her on her return from a recent careers convention. But she wasn't. She'd done it all now – she'd been through the whole process of hanging on to her old self, carving out patches of time, not relinquishing her work, then partly letting go in order to be more with the children, his work taking precedence over hers as generally seemed to be the case when the parents were still together. Unless the woman earned more, which opened up a whole new can of modern worms. Those long-forgotten hours and days were now like nourishing leaf mould round their roots. Let the past go (sang Zoe beneath her breath), time to move on; her own built-in obsolescence could make her feel lively rather than sad. And perhaps the shape of life would be like an hour-glass, clear and wide to begin with, narrowing down to the tunnel of the middle years, then flaring wide again before the sands ran out.

'Mum, can you test me on my words?' asked George. He was doing a French taster term, taking it seriously because he wanted to outstrip his friend Mick who was better than him at maths.

'Well I'm not supposed to,' said Zoe. 'But we're not moving. Here, put it on my lap and keep your eye open for when the car in front starts to move.'

When I was starting out, leaving babies till after thirty was seen as leaving it late (thought Zoe). Over thirty was the time of fade for women, loss of bloom and all that. Now you're expected to be still a girl at forty-two – slim, active, up for it. But if I hadn't done it, had Joe at twenty-six and Theresa at twenty-eight, hammered away at work and sweated blood in pursuit of good childminders, nurseries, au pairs, you name it, and finally, five years later when George came along, slowed down for a while at least; then I wouldn't know why so many women are the way they are. Stymied at some point; silenced somewhere. Stalled. Or, merely delayed?

'It's who, when, where, how and all that sort of thing,' said George. 'I'll tell you how I remember *quand*. I think of the Sorcerer's Apprentice, because you know he had a WAND, rhymes with *quand*, and then he goes away with all those buckets of water and then WHEN he comes back . . . Get it? WHEN he comes back! That's how it stays in my mind. And *qui* is the KEY in a door and you answer it and who is there? WHO! I thought of all that myself, yeah. Course. And *où* is monkeys in the rainforest. Oo oo oo. Hey look, it's moving.'

They crawled forward, even getting into second gear for a few seconds, then settled again into stasis.

'Why the rainforest?' asked Zoe. 'Monkeys in the rainforest?'

'Because, WHERE are they?' he asked. 'Where *are* they, the trees in the rainforest. That's what the monkeys want to know, oo oo oo. Cos they aren't there any more, the trees in the rainforest.'

'You remember everything they teach you at school, don't you,' said Zoe admiringly.

'Just about,' said George with a pleased smile. 'Mum, I don't want you to die until I'm grown up.'

There was a pause.

'But I don't want to die *before* you,' he added.

'No, I don't want that either,' said Zoe.

This boy remembers every detail of every unremarkable day (thought Zoe); he's not been alive that long and he's got acres of lovely empty space in his memory bank. Whereas I've been alive for ages and it's got to the point where my mind is saying it already has enough on its shelves, it just can't be bothered to store something new unless it's *really* worth remembering.

I climb the stairs and forget what I'm looking for. I forgot to pick up Natasha last week when I'd promised her mother, and I had to do a three-point turn in the middle of Ivanhoe Avenue and go back for her and just hope that none of the children already in the car would snitch on me. But that's nothing new. I can't remember a thing about the last decade or so, she told other mothers, and they agreed, it was a blur, a blank; they had photographs to prove it had happened, but they couldn't remember it themselves. She, Zoe, saw her memory banks as having shrivelled for lack of sleep's welcome rain; she brooded over the return of those refreshing showers and the rehydration of her pot-noodle bundles of memories, and how (one day) the past would plump into action, swelling with import, newly alive.

When she was old and free and in her second adolescence, she would sleep in royally, till midday or one. Yet old people cannot revisit that country, they report; they wake and listen to the dawn chorus after four or five threadbare hours, and long for the old three-ply youth-giving slumber.

They had reached Freda's house, and Zoe stopped the car to let George out. He went off to ring the bell and wait while Freda and also Harry, who was in on this lift, gathered their bags and shoes and coats. It was too narrow a road to hover in, or rather Zoe did not have the nerve to make other people queue behind her while she waited for her passengers to arrive. This morning she shoehorned the car into a minute space three hundred yards away, proudly parking on a sixpence.

What's truly radical now though (thought Zoe, rereading the text from Amy as she waited) is to imagine a man and woman having children and living happily together, justice and love prevailing, self-respect on both sides, each making sure the other flourishes as well as the children. The windscreen blurred as it started to rain. If not constantly, she modified, then taking turns. Where *are* they?

But this wave of divorces (she thought), the couples who'd had ten or fifteen years or more of being together, her feeling was that often it wasn't as corny as it seemed to be in Amy's case – being left for youth. When she, Zoe, looked closely, it was more to do with the mercurial resentment quotient present in every marriage having risen to the top of the thermometer. It was more to do with how

When she was old and free and in her second adolescence, she would sleep in royally, till midday or one

the marriage had turned out, now it was this far down the line. Was one of the couple thriving and satisfied, with the other restless or foundering? Or perhaps the years had spawned a marital Black Dog, where one of them dragged the other down with endless gloom or bad temper or censoriousness and refused to be comforted, ever, and also held the other responsible for their misery.

There had been a scattering of bust-ups during the first two or three years of having babies, and then things seemed to settle down. This was the second wave, a decade or so on, a wild tsunami of divorce as children reached adolescence and parents left youth behind. The third big wave was set to come when the children left home. She, Zoe, had grown familiar with the process simply by listening. First came the shock, the vulnerability and hurt; then the nastiness (particularly about money) with accompanying baffled incredulity; down on to indignation at the exposure of unsuspected talents for treachery, secretiveness, two-faced liardom; falling last of all into scalding grief or adamantine hatred. Only last week her next door neighbour, forced to put the house on the market, had hissed at her over the fence, 'I hope he gets cancer and dies.' Though when it came to showing round prospective purchasers, the estate agents always murmured the word 'amicable' as reassurance; purchasers wanted to hear it was amicable rather than that other divorce word, acrimonious.

She peered into the driver's mirror and saw them trudging towards her with their usual heaps of school luggage. It was still well before eight and, judging herself more bleached and craggy than usual, she added some colour just as they got to the car.

'Lipstick, hey,' said George, taking the front seat. The other two shuffled themselves and their bags into the back.

'I used to wear make-up,' said Zoe. 'Well, a bit. When I was younger. I really enjoyed it.'

'Why don't you now?' asked Freda. Freda's mother did, of course. Her mother was thirty-eight rather than forty-two. It made a difference, this slide over to the other side, reflected Zoe, and also one was tireder.

'Well, I still do if I feel like it,' she said, starting the car and indicating. She waited for a removal van to lumber along and shave past. 'But I don't do it every day like brushing my teeth. It's just another thing.' Also, nobody but you lot is going to see me so why would I, she added silently, churlishly.

She was aware of the children thinking, what? *Why* not? Women *should* wear make-up. Freda in particular would be on the side of glamour and looking one's best at all times.

'We had a Mexican student staying with us once,' she told them, edging onto the main road. 'And at first she would spend ages looking after her long glossy hair, and more ages brushing make-up onto her eyelids and applying that gorgeous glassy lipgloss. But after a while she stopped, and she looked just like the rest of us – she said to me that it was a lovely holiday after Mexico City, where she really couldn't go outside without the full works or everybody would stare at her. So she kept it for parties or times when she felt like putting it on, after that.'

'Women look better with make-up,' commented Harry from the back. Harry's mother dropped him off at Freda's on Tuesday and Thursday mornings, and, in the spirit of hawk-eyed reciprocity on which the whole fragile school-run ecosystem was founded, Zoe collected George from Harry's house on Monday and Wednesday afternoons, which cut *that* journey in half.

'Well I'm always going to wear make-up when I'm older,' said Freda.

'Women used to set their alarm clocks an hour early so they could put on their false eyelashes and lid liner and all that,' said Zoe. 'Imagine being frightened of your husband seeing your bare face!'

There was silence as they considered this, grudging assent, even. But the old advice was still doing the rounds, Zoe had noticed, for women to listen admiringly to men and not to laugh at them if they wanted to snare one of their very own. Give a man respect for being higher caste than you, freer, more powerful. And men, what was it men wanted? Was it true they only wanted a cipher? That a woman should not expect admiration from a man for any other qualities than physical beauty or selflessness? Surely not. If this were the case, why live with such a poor sap if you could scrape your own living?

'Do you like Alex?' asked Harry. 'I don't. I hate Alex, he whines and he's mean and he cries and he whinges all the time. But I pretend I like him, because I want him to like me.'

There was no comment from the other three. They were sunk in early-morning torpor, staring at the static traffic around them.

'I despise him,' said Harry.

'You can't say that,' said Freda. 'It's despise.'

'That's what I said,' said Harry.

George snorted.

It was nothing short of dangerous and misguided (thought Zoe) not to keep earning, even if it wasn't very much and you were doing all the domestic and emotional work as well, for the sake of keeping the marital Black Dog at bay. Otherwise if you spoke up it would be like biting the hand that fed you. Yes you wanted to be around (thought Zoe), to be an armoire, to make them safe as houses. But surrendering your autonomy for too long, subsumption without promise of future release, those weren't good for the health.

'I hate that feeling in the playground when I've bullied someone and then they start crying,' said Harry with candour.

'I don't like it if someone cries because of something I've said,' said Freda.

'I don't like it when there's a group of people and they're making someone cry,' said George over his shoulder. 'That makes me feel bad.'

'Oh I don't mind that,' said Harry. 'If it wasn't me that

made them cry. If it was other people, that's nothing to do with me.'

'No, but don't you feel bad when you see one person like that,' replied George, 'and everyone picking on them, if you don't, like, say something?'

'No,' said Harry. 'I don't care. As long as *I'm* not being nasty to them I don't feel bad at what's happening.'

'Oh,' said George, considering. 'I do.'

'Look at that car's number plate,' said Freda. 'The letters say XAN. XAN! XAN!'

'FWMM!' joined in Harry. 'FWMMFWMM! FWM-MFWMMFWMM!'

'BGA,' growled George. 'BGA. Can you touch your nose with your tongue?'

Zoe stared out from the static car at the line of people waiting in the rain at a bus stop, and studied their faces. Time sinks into flesh (she mused), gradually sinks it. A look of distant bruising arrives, and also for some reason asymmetry. One eye sits higher than the other and the mouth looks crooked. We start to resemble cartoons or caricatures of ourselves. On cold days like today the effect can be quite trollish.

'Who would you choose to push off a cliff or send to prison or give a big hug?' George threw over his shoulder. 'Out of three – Peter Vallings—'

'Ugh, not Peter Vallings!' shrieked Freda in an ecstasy of disgust.

'Mrs Campbell. And – Mr Starling!'

'Mr Starling! Oh my God, Mr Starling,' said Harry, caught between spasms of distaste and delight. 'Yesterday he was wearing this top, yeah, he lets you see how many ripples he's got.'

Your skin won't stay with your flesh as it used to (thought Zoe); it won't move and follow muscle the way it did before. You turn, and there is a fan of creases however trim you are; yet once you were one of these young things at the bus stop, these over-eleven secondary school pupils. Why do we smile at adolescent boys, so unfinished, so lumpy (she wondered) but feel disturbed by this early beauty of the girls, who gleam with benefit, their hair smooth as glass or in rich ringlets, smiling big smiles and speaking up and nobody these days saying, 'Who do you think you are?' or 'You look like a prostitute.' It's not as if the boys won't catch up with a vengeance.

'I love my dog,' said Harry fiercely.

'Yes, he's a nice dog,' agreed Freda.

'I love my dog so much,' continued Harry, 'I would rather die than see my dog die.'

'*You* would rather die than your *dog*?' said George in disbelief.

'Yes! I love my dog! Don't you love *your* dog?'

'Yes. But . . .'

'You don't really love your dog. If you wouldn't die instead of him.'

Zoe bit her tongue. Her rule was, never join in. That way they could pretend she wasn't there. The sort of internal monologue she enjoyed these days came from being round older children, at their disposal but silent. She was able to dip in and out of her thoughts now with the freedom of a bird. Whereas it was true enough that no thought could take wing round the under-fives; what they needed was too constant and minute and demanding, you had to be out of the room in order to think and they needed you *in* the room.

When George walked beside her he liked to hold on to what he called her elbow flab. He pinched it till it held a separate shape. He was going to be tall. As high as my heart, she used to say last year, but he had grown since then; he came up to her shoulder now, this nine-year-old.

'Teenagers!' he'd said to her not long ago. 'When I turn thirteen I'll be horrible in one night. Covered in spots and rude to you and not talking. Jus' grunting.'

Where did he get all that from? The most difficult age for girls was fourteen, they now claimed, the parenting experts, while for boys it was nineteen. Ten more years then. Good.

'Would you like to be tall?' she'd asked him that time.

'Not very,' he'd said decisively. 'But I wouldn't like just to be five eight or something. I'd want to be taller than my wife.'

His *wife*! Some way down the corridor of the years, she saw his wife against the fading sun, her face in shade. Would his wife mind if she, Zoe, hugged him when they met? She might, she might well. More than the father giving away his daughter, the mother must hand over her son. Perhaps his *wife* would only allow them to shake hands. When he was little his hands had been like velvet, without knuckles or veins; he used to put his small warm hands up her cardigan sleeves when he was wheedling for something.

They were inching their way down Mordred Hill, some sort of delay having been caused by a juggernaut trying to back into an eighteenth-century alley centimetres too narrow for it. Zoe sighed with disbelief, then practised her deep breathing. Nothing you could do about it, no point in road rage, the country was stuffed to the gills with cars and that was all there was to it. She had taken the Civil Service exams after college and one of the questions had been, 'How would you arrange the transport system of this country?' At the time, being utterly wrapped up in cliometrics and dendrochronology, she had been quite unable to answer; but now, a couple of decades down the line, she felt fully qualified to write several thousand impassioned words, if not a thesis, on the subject.

But then if you believe in wives and steadfastness and heroic monogamy (thought Zoe, as the lorry cleared the space and the traffic began to flow again), how can you admit change? Her sister Valerie had described how she was making her husband read aloud each night in bed from *How to Rescue a Relationship*. When he protested, she pointed out that it was instead of going to a marriage guidance counsellor. Whoever wants to live must forget, Valerie had told her drily; that was the gist of it. She, Zoe,

wasn't sure that she would be able to take marriage guidance counselling seriously either, as she suspected it was
probably done mainly by women who were no longer
needed on the school run. It all seemed to be about
women needed and wanted, then not needed and not
wanted. She moved off in second gear.

No wonder there were gaggles of mothers sitting over
milky lattes all over the place from 8.40 a.m. They were
recovering from driving exclusively in the first two gears
for the last hour; they had met the school deadline and
now wanted some pleasure on the return run. Zoe pre-
ferred her own company at this time of the morning, and
also did not relish the conversation of such groups, which
tended to be fault-finding sessions on how Miss Scantle-
bury taught long division or post-mortems on reported
classroom injustices, bubblings-up of indignation and the
urge to interfere, still to be the main moving force in their
child's day. She needed a coffee though – a double mac-
chiato, to be precise – and she liked the café sensation of
being alone but in company, surrounded by tables of
huddled intimacies each hived off from the other, scraps of
conversation drifting in the air. Yesterday, she remembered, there had been those two women in baggy velour
tracksuits at the table nearest to her, very solemn.

'I feel rather protective towards him. The girls are very
provocative the way they dress now. He's thirteen.'

'Especially when you're surrounded by all these images.
Everywhere you go.'

'It's not a very nice culture.'

'No, it's not.'

And all around there had been that steady self-justificatory hum of women telling each other the latest version of themselves, their lives, punctuated with the occasional righteous cry as yet another patch of moral high ground was claimed. That's a real weakness (she thought, shaking her head), and an enemy of, of – whatever it is we're after. Amity, would you call it?

'Last year when we were in Cornwall we went out in a boat and we saw sharks,' said Harry.

'Sharks!' scoffed George. 'Ho yes. In *Cornwall*.'

'No, really,' insisted Harry.

'It's eels as well,' said Freda. 'I don't like them either.'

'Ooh no,' Harry agreed, shuddering.

'What about sea-snakes,' said George. 'They can swim into any hole in your body.'

The car fell silent as they absorbed this information.

'Where did you hear this?' asked Zoe suspiciously; she had her own reservations about Mr Starling.

'Mr Starling told us,' smirked George. 'If it goes in at your ear, you're dead because it sneaks into your brain. But if it goes up your . . .'

'What happens if it gets in up there?' asked Harry.

'If it gets in there, up inside you,' said George, 'you don't die but they have to take you to hospital and cut you open and pull it out.'

The talk progressed naturally from here to tapeworms.

'They hang on to you by hooks all the way down,' said Harry. 'You have to poison them, by giving the person enough to kill the worm but not them. Then the worm dies and the hooks get loose and the worm comes out. Either of your bottom or somehow they pull it through your mouth.'

'That's enough of that,' said Zoe at last. 'It's too early in the morning.'

They reached the road where the school was with five minutes to spare, and Zoe drew in to the kerb some way off while they decanted their bags and shoes and morning selves. Would George kiss her? She only got a kiss when they arrived if none of the boys in his class was around. He knew she wanted a kiss, and gave her a warning look. No, there was Sean McIlroy – no chance today.

They were gone. The car was suddenly empty, she sat unkissed, redundant, cast off like an old boot. 'Boohoo,' she murmured, her eyes blurring for a moment, and carefully adjusted her wing mirror for something to do.

Then George reappeared, tapping at the window, looking stern and furtive.

'I said I'd forgotten my maths book,' he muttered when she opened the car door, and, leaning across as though to pick up something from the seat beside her, smudged her cheek with a hurried – but (thought Zoe) unsurpassable – kiss.

© Celia Clark

Helen Simpson writes sharply funny, brilliantly observed short stories, and with each of her six collections, one published every five years since *Four Bare Legs in a Bed* in 1990, she has been hailed as a 'contemporary maestro of the short story' (*Sunday Times*) and 'a wry, humane and brilliant observer of our peculiar condition' (*Independent*). In the introduction to the Vintage Classics selection of her work, *A Bunch of Fives*, Simpson addresses the fact that many of her stories deal with 'baby stuff', pointing out there was very little in print about it when her earliest collections were published – another example of how her stories are ground-breaking while remaining rooted in every-day life. She has also said she is 'interested in how men and women (and children) live together. Or don't.'

Before writing her first stories, Helen Simpson was a staff writer at *Vogue* and published two cookery books. She lives in London, and her latest collection is *Cockfosters* (2015).

RECOMMENDED BOOKS BY HELEN SIMPSON:

Dear George
Hey Yeah Right Get a Life
Constitutional
A Bunch of Fives
In-Flight Entertainment

How do we survive Motherhood?

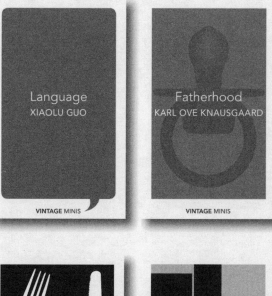

VINTAGE MINIS

The Vintage Minis bring you the world's greatest writers on the experiences that make us human. These stylish, entertaining little books explore the whole spectrum of life – from birth to death, and everything in between. Which means there's something here for everyone, whatever your story.

vintageminis.co.uk